Cover design by Melanie Stephens
Front and back cover by Melanie Stephens

All artwork featured in the novel
By Eliza Stephens and Authors own

The attempted demise of Augusta Walsh
Age 15 years, 4 months, and 6 days

By Melanie Stephens

This book is dedicated to every teenager on the planet. You are our Earth's future. Be brave, embrace you, and continue to grow that little seed of brilliance hidden within.

Name: Augusta Walsh
Age: 15 years, 3 weeks.
Write what's on my mind: My mind is empty.
Write what I see and feel: I am invisible.

I look out the window, and no one knows I'm here. The world moves tiptoeing around me as I sit still and silent. People are oblivious. They all have somewhere to go, something to do. Yet, I have no purpose, no plans- lost without a map with no sense of direction of where I'm supposed to be.

My stomach hurts.

Cars are moving outside like nothing has happened yet in my home; it is THE ONLY thing that has happened. Everyone is watching, waiting for reasons, wondering if it will happen again. My mum calls it my 'blip'; apparently, it's unbearable to say the word suicide or attempt. She is downstairs making me Nutella on toast. Mum made a point of promising me no crusts- announcing it like it was monumental, the answer to all our prayers. She treats me like this little toddler kid who can't use a knife!

This notebook was her idea. The Doctor suggested writing as a therapy tool to get rid of nasty thoughts, so Mum immediately drove into town and bought this notebook and a pack of blue Bic biros so I could start right away.

When the Doctor recommended taking a bath as a stress buster, she returned with bath bombs and lavender oil. When he said to try and exercise regularly, she told me she bought us all memberships to the local leisure centre-
gym, swimming, and classes. By that, I mean me, Mum, and Mac (who also lives with us). Her idea was we do it all together. However, Mac already goes to a gym- a different one- why did she think he would need access to two? Mac, of course, said nothing about it, but when she left the room, he said, "Your mum is only trying to help in any way she can."

Which I get, but the thought of being in a swimming costume in front of people fills me with dread. Sweating on treadmills, rowing machines, and exercise bikes, looking weak, going all puffy and red surrounded by flawless bodies- it would be a nightmare!

"Think of this notebook as your friend to whom you can tell everything. So, write in it daily, anything on your mind, what you see, how you feel, no matter how big or small."

This is what Mum told me when she gave me this. I don't know if every day will be possible- I mean, I have things to do, places to go, people to see. I'm just not doing anything right now. The truth is I'm a bit scared of leaving my bedroom. It's a small room, but it's mine, and for the time being, I need my things, my space, and my world. My own little refuge from an overprotective family who won't let up.

I have no phone- Mum took it away. So, I have no idea what's happening in the world, no connection to people from school, and no clue what anyone's doing this summer. I am living in the dark ages.

The Doctor's suggested I come off social media for a bit, so Mum said she'd take my phone and look after it for me. Only for a little while whilst I recover. I'm not sure how watching people do TikTok dances or sharing photos of themselves on holiday would tip me over the edge, but he's the expert.

So that is why I am writing. I have nothing else to do. So, let's see, what's on my mind?

 Nope, nothing. Still empty.

What do I see? Grass, road, pavement.

 Outside there is a massive dog whose owner is short, like a midget or a tiny little Oompa Loompa- it looks so weird. On the other hand, maybe the dog is standard and only looks gigantic because the person is so small.

What do I feel:
Fed up. Bored. Maybe a little peckish. I'm craving my Nutella on toast now, with the crusts off, and an ice lolly if we got one. And my phone. I want my phone. I need it before I do something drastic, like go random and paint my hands blue for no reason whatsoever. At least it would make life a little bit more interesting. Finally, I can hear Mum bringing up my toast. Starving.

Thursday morning, 22nd August.
My best friend, Dakota has messaged me
on WhatsApp and asked if I want to come
over. Mum told her about my 'blip'.

I haven't seen anyone since the hospital- it's only
been Mum, Dad, and Mac for weeks. I looked in the mirror,
and I didn't look right. If I go over to her place, she will
want to talk about it, and I definitely don't want to. I
want to forget it's happened for a bit and for people to act
normal around me again.

"Augusta, are you going to go?"

Mum stood there in the kitchen as I answered
Dakota.

"No," I replied as I tapped the keyboard, wondering
why my fingers were so fat. It takes me ages because the
predictive text is constantly changing words. Even real ones!
My message went from 'Thanks, but I'm going to chill at
home. Relax for a bit. X' to 'Thanks bus I'm jolly google to
call act home. Relate from a bike, X' I mean, what on Earth
is that?

"Don't you think it might be good for you guys to
catch up? Maybe get out of the house for a bit?' Mum
pressed while wiping down the kitchen doors. She looked at
me and did a double take. "Why are your hands blue?"

I handed the phone back to Mum and shrugged.
"That's okay. We'll hang out another time." And I came
back upstairs.

Dakota and I have known each other since primary school. She's the only person I know who actually likes my name. Even I don't. My mum says Augusta is prestigious. Long ago, it was a title of honour given to wives and daughters of mighty Roman Emperors; it means Great, Magnificent. But all I see when I think of the name Augusta is 'Augusta Disgusta'. On my first day of school, I was given that nickname. I had no chance. From the start, I was doomed.

But, when I first told Dakota on the day we met, she said, "Augusta is like being called August, which is my favourite month!" She explained there's no school, and her birthday is in August (I missed it this year because of the 'blip'. Mum sent a card and some money over along with a tray of brownies, her favourite dessert.).

Dakota also thought it was cool to have a name that made people think of last summer when everyone was happy. Oh, the irony! Augusta defines happiness. What a joke!

Dakota finally had her ears done this summer. They're pierced, but she has wanted to have them done at the top part for over a year. I can't remember what it's called, and unfortunately, I can't Google it cause Mum has my phone. The ear piercings were a birthday present from her dad. It would be nice to see them, but I haven't got the energy for any company right now. She also wants to get a tattoo but can't before she's 18. Apparently, it's the law. So, on her 18th birthday, we decided we would get matching tattoos. I like drawing so I said I would design something. It would have to represent us both well, so we don't regret it when we're 50. I haven't thought about what it will be yet, but I have time to think about it.

This afternoon I saw my dad. I think Mum called him because I wasn't going to Dakotas. At first, he was sitting in our lounge for ages, so Mum told him to take me out. We decided to go to McDonald's.

After we placed our order, we were just waiting, neither of us saying anything. It was really uncomfortable. I was really bored, so I took the straw from its paper packet and folded the end to make a kind of point. I scratched the top of my finger and cleaned dirt from beneath my fingernails. The straw is paper too, so I wondered if I could pierce the skin on my fingertip and essentially give myself a paper cut. My dad watched me looking more and more uneasy. I could see the frowned eyebrow look becoming more and more prominent the longer we had to wait.

My dad let himself go and seems really old now. Mum takes care of herself a bit- goes to the hairdressers, works out, and drinks smoothies. She's had the same haircut for as long as I can remember. It's the Rachel cut- it comes from a show called *Friends*. I haven't seen it, but I think they show it on Netflix. They sell t-shirts of the show in Primark and H&M, so it's still popular, maybe a bit retro. Mum always tells me, "I'll have you know; people were lined around the block to get this done not too long ago."

I have to tell her, "Mum, that was the 90s which was like 30 years ago!!!"

I can't imagine her hair any different now. But my dad's barnet looks a mess. He's fat, thinning on top, only a few strands of his sandy hair poking through his bald head, and his skin has that dimpled effect. Not a good look. He never used to be like that, but he's gone downhill.

Our food finally came. It felt as if we had been waiting for days. I ate, chewed, and swallowed; I didn't even taste it. This family was opposite us, and this snotty little kid was staring at me. He had this look on his face like I was an alien or something. I stared at him back and did that thing where you make your eyeballs bigger to intimidate him, but he kept doing it and watched me eat the whole time. I felt conscious of every mouthful. Finally, I looked away, but he was still doing it when I turned back.

"Dad, that kid keeps staring at me."

 My dad jumped a little. He always does whenever anything happens. It's like Dad thinks he's in the war or something and keeps expecting a bomb to drop. But he's never been near one. Dad turned, looked at the bug-eyed little weirdo and no word of a lie; HE SAW HIM STARING and said,

"Don't be silly, Augusta. I'm sure he has better things to do than stare at a complete stranger."

HE SAW HIM DOING IT!!!!!!!! What the hell, Dad?

On the way back, he spent the whole time asking me about Mum and Mac. I wish he'd move on; he's fixated on the past and when we were together. Mac is the complete opposite of Dad. He's younger than Mum, not older like Dad, but it doesn't look too weird cause Mum is young for her age. They met at the hospital, Mum is a Community Paediatrician, and Mac is a bereavement Councillor. With his job, Mac works from home quite a bit which he likes. My dad is a finance manager in an office. He's worked in the same firm since I was born. Dad doesn't even like his job much, but he's not overly confident. Dad's unsure what else he could do. I always tell him to try something new, but Dad says his pension is built up now, and he doesn't want to lose it by starting over again.

Mac lifts weights: you can see his muscles through his clothes. He and Mum are in an inter-racial relationship which she was worried about at first with Gran and stuff as she's pretty old-fashioned and ancient but a complete menace. So, she is always saying inappropriate things. But nothing happened. Gran said, "Bloody hell! He looks like one of those Dreamboys they keep having in the hall!". Which made Mum go bright red and immediately apologised to Mac about her Mum comparing him to a male stripper. Mac thought it was funny, I thought it was cringe. I'm happy about Gran being okay with it though because I like Mac. He listens to me and takes in what I'm saying.

When I talk about stuff, people often act like I don't know anything. That I can't possibly comprehend or contribute any positive impact because I'm only 15. But people can be  set on ways of doing things for no other reason than they have always been done that way and never consider any other options. There are a lot of adults dumber than a 15, and 16-year-old kid. We can think of solutions, be creative, and present new perspectives. Maybe we don't know everything there is to know about one subject, but we can think outside the box. You never know; our ideas might work and make things better.

Look at Climate Change, Global Warming. People are so used to doing the same things in their daily routines that they refuse to make any changes, no matter the cost to us, their kids, and the Earth. They continue polluting the air oblivious about its effect on the planet. The government aren't doing anywhere near enough to take control of the problem. Instead, their neglect continues to present a grim outlook for humanity, especially my generation and any future ones. I don't even know if I want children, neither do any of my friends. What will happen to the natural world and its ecosystem? Every living thing and being relies on air.

We're trying to speak up, but we are being ignored. We have to live longer before we are adequate enough to form any valuable insights, yet it is our fate that is becoming more and more uncertain. It is our world that is being destroyed. Innocence is not  ignorance. If they know everything, and we know nothing, how can we see it and they don't? Being unaware is not the same as conscious deafness over reasoning and insight. So, why don't they stop cutting down trees, relying so much on cars, and actually concentrate on how to save us and heal our Earth?

Like I say, Mac listens to me and invites me into conversations with people like I have value and something interesting to say. Dad gets along with him but always asks if Mum and Mac are happy, whether they argue, and what kind of things they do together. If it was anyone else, I would tell him to mind his own business, but it is my dad, and he just took me to McDonald's, so I said, "Don't know" to almost every question. Finally, he got the message and stopped asking me about them. Parents can be so annoying!

Friday 28th August

Finally, Mum's given me back my phone, so I messaged Dakota to see if she wanted to hang out for a bit. She still hasn't answered, so I looked on WhatsApp to see if the ticks were blue, confirming she's seen it.

It was sent 18 minutes ago, which is ages. So I went on info, and I saw Dakota had read it, so obviously, she doesn't want to deal with me or talk to me.

I don't know if she still wants to be my friend. Maybe I'm too much of a burden to hang out with- unwelcome drama. Dakota obviously doesn't want to see me. Perhaps she thinks I'll cry, get hysterical or do something terrible and make things awkward, or mad at me for not coming to her house last week.

It took 23 minutes, but eventually she messaged back. She's at the hairdressers with her sister. I didn't even know Dakota regularly went to the hairdressers. Her hair is thick and really fuzzy, it never looks styled- should I go and get my hair done too? Or maybe this is an excuse, so she doesn't have to see me. That's probably more plausible. Who knows if I even have a best friend anymore?

Dakota messaged again, and I think she is telling me the truth. She said that Ellie, her sister, took her there as a big treat before returning to school, and she would see me after the holidays. I wonder what Dakota's having done. She has this mass of curly hair; there's not much you can do with it.

I can't believe we are going to be in our final year. It's both scary because this means exams and I have to decide which college I want to attend, but also exciting because we can finally leave school and be seniors. The cool ones, the untouchables. I remember when I first started- as a year 7- I saw the year 11's as this elite gang I would never be a part of. Now we'll be the superior pupils with enormous responsibilities. I can't wait to get school over with. It will

be nice to not have any rules, to do our own thing.

I picked up my sketchbook yesterday, the first time since my 'blip'. A nurse at the hospital was really nice, she asked me what I liked to do, and I said I draw. She told me it was a brilliant skill to have, as it could help me along with the writing and be another way to get my thoughts down. Art therapy is a massive thing for working through emotions, apparently.

I haven't felt the urge to do any art before now, but
I need to build my portfolio GCSE anyway. So, I guess if I
can draw as art therapy and get some schoolwork done
simultaneously it's pretty cool.

The piece I did was a tunnel with a tiny circle of
light at the end. Along the bottom was dark water with
subtle wispy glimmers under a rickety boat in the middle.
The little wooden rowboat has no oars, so there is nothing
to stop it from heading toward the tunnel. I'm in the boat.
The tunnel's walls have sharp pointy rocks with dried
droplets of blood in dark deep moody red. I used charcoal
because I wanted to show the black and darkness of the
water and tunnel.

I worked on adding texture and tone to the rocks and water all day. The boat I kept simple but worn so it looked like it wouldn't survive the journey. I slowly tore my picture off the wire spine and put it safely in the bottom of my chest of drawers. A hand towel I had taken from the airing cupboard was placed on top so the charcoal wouldn't stain my hoodies. I'm not ready to show anyone yet. Exposing my vulnerability like that takes me time to work up to. One day I might be brave enough, but certainly not today.

Thursday 3rd September

It's only a few days before school, so Mum and Mac took me to town for some new supplies to get me excited about going back. I told Mum about Ellie taking Dakota to the hairdressers as she asked me why we weren't hanging out anymore. As usual, it was my fault. Mum started lecturing me about shutting people out, so I showed her I had tried, that, in fact, it was Dakota who didn't want to hang out with me.

Mum was quiet for a minute, giving my ears a rest from all the moaning. Then she asked me, "Do you want to go to the hairdressers too? Have a bit of a treat and tidy up?"

I shrugged. I didn't care. My hair is long, limp, dull and straight. And brown, the most boring colour. I would like to get some bright colours into it, so it makes it more interesting, but Mum doesn't like the idea of chemicals being in my hair, so I'm not allowed. When I'm 18, I can do what I want, so I'm going to shave half of it off, right down the middle. On the other side of my head, I'll have it reach my jawline and gradually get shorter toward the back. I've seen pictures of it online, and it looks incredible. There will be patterns like scrolling in the shaved bit and a thick stripe of colour down the front. It's going to be stellar.

As my hair is so uninteresting and flat, I rarely do anything with it apart from putting it up in a ponytail or letting it hang lifeless around my shoulders and back. Some girls instinctively know how to do their hair, always looking good, but that's not me. I hate how it looks but I don't know how to fix it.

Mum took me to her usual salon for a cut and blow-dry, while Mac went to pick up his contact lenses at the optician. Mum told the hairdresser, a heavy blonde woman (who didn't have great hair herself, to be honest), to freshen things up. I don't think Mum knows what to do with it either.

I have never had a shampoo before. Of course, I wash my hair, it's not dripping in grease, and I don't have dreadlocks or anything, but I mean at a salon. My head went in this tiny helmet sink, and she rubbed stuff in. I could feel her long fingernails raking through my hair. I didn't like the position she put me in. I kept pulling my hoodie loose around my chest. My breasts are abnormally massive. I've worn bras since the summer before year 7. I hate them, and people stare. The hairdresser woman was looking at them now. I felt her eyes on me as her nails continued to scratch my scalp.

"Try not to fidget so much, sweetheart." I don't like her voice.

"Augusta, stay still!" Mum again treating me like I'm 8 years old.

Between the blonde fingernail-happy hairdresser and my mother, the people in the salon were now fixed in my direction. I couldn't see them, but I could feel everyone watching me, and I wanted up, away from the helmet sink, but my hair was wet, and I looked stupid.

She stopped the water, put my hair in a turban, and held it as we did this strange awkward scuffle to a chair. I sat with a thump, and the woman and Mum chatted as she began to snip. Mum chats to everyone. It's really annoying.

I have no idea how she knows what to say to people. The hairdresser tried asking me the usual nonsense- when they have no idea how to speak to a 15-year-old.

"Are you looking forward to going back to school?" (I shrugged. A bit.)

"What year are you in?" (11- this is typically followed by oh, we didn't have year 11 in my day. It was all juniors, a bar of soap, and straight to work.)

"Do you like school?" (Who does, really)

"Do you have lots of friends?" (Who cares)

It always amuses me that these are the questions out of everything about me that adults want to know. I'm not exactly sure what they say about me or what kind of person I am. So why not ask me something a bit more interesting? Maybe so I can talk freely or show a slither of personality?

-What do I like to do?

-Do I enjoy music or films? If so, what am I into?

-If I had three wishes, what would I choose?

-Where in the world would I like to visit?

-If I had to choose between having one arm or a face made of jelly, which would I choose?

After my uninteresting one-word answers to lame and predictable questions, the hairdresser gave up. Instead, she concentrated on Mum, along with this old woman who sat in the chair beside mine. All three of them were laughing, talking about roadworks and unaffordable housing. I wonder what age, as a grown-up, you begin to care about this stuff? It's so painstakingly dull.

It's ridiculous to me how much adults care about the weather. They always talk about it! They can't resist! Yet, nothing they say will change it. What a waste of air and unnecessary noise. Nonetheless, they speak to everyone about it, even strangers! It's the first thing they say! Why? Who cares if it's due to rain next week or it gets sunnier?

Usually, they are outside experiencing the weather with the person mundanely agreeing with them. Where do they get their information from to make all these future predictions? No one asks. Instead, they talk about the weatherman; as if all other experts are wrong, even the MET office. It astounds me how everyone keeps all the hard stuff, and things they need to talk about to stay sane. However, they discuss the weather to anyone, as it's of the uttermost importance!

I know I don't talk about any important stuff either, which is why I'm so messed up but never have I said, "nice weather". I don't know how much captivation or fascination adults genuinely have about the weather. I would like to know. I'm intrigued if they genuinely don't know what else to say to each other.

I wonder if awkwardness and inadequate social skills never actually leave you. When you are older, are you still petrified of trusting another person? Or to be completely open by exposing what you are really thinking about. Either that or they are like robots and used to having the same conversations over and over, like a weird sociable reflex. A bit like conditioning and Pavlov's dog. But instead of a bell, it's the mere presence of another person.

After the hairdresser had blow-dried my hair, I actually quite liked it.

The nail equivalent of Edward Scissorhands asked if I wanted my hair curled for a change, so I'd look more grown up. I think she was thinking mature, but I was thinking poodle, so I said no, thank you. So instead, she straightened it and brought out all the layers she had put in. I ran my fingers through after she finished, and my whole hair felt lighter than air. Weightless. It's never felt that way before.

Mac came into the salon halfway through the straightening and praised it after it was done.
After we left, he said I looked great, and there was only one way to treat such a pretty lady. Pancakes with lashings of maple syrup! He always wants to eat out and indulge, it's fun going shopping with him. Mac took Mum and me to one of our favourite haunts, where they also do proper milkshakes with ice cream and Oreos. Mum stuck to coffee and a toasted teacake, but Mac and I went for it! I was so full after. Mum said all that sugar reminded her she needs to book the dentist next week. I think that sounded funnier in her head, or she may have been serious. You can't always tell with Mum! Mac laughed, but he always does at her jokes no matter how bad they are.

Mum said we still need to get me a new pencil case, but I told her my old one was fine. She also suggested art supplies, as the Art shop is just next door to the café. It seemed like a nice idea, and a chance to get more stuff.

Overall, it was a good day and made me almost a little excited to return to school. I want to show everyone my new hair and see how they react.

I am a bit worried people will know what's happened regarding my 'blip'. It's a bit scary when I think about that. It makes me incredibly nervous. My hand begins to quiver, and I have to sit on it. The school could throw me out if they knew, or think I need a special needs school or mental hospital, and I don't want to miss my final year. People would sing songs about being crazy in the corridors, and most likely campaign, or start a movement to try and get me out, so they don't have to look at me or be near to me. As far as I'm aware only Dakota knows. That is how it must stay. I really hope they don't see it on my face and guess.

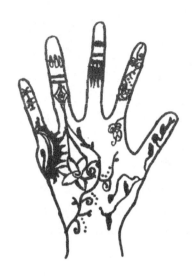

Monday 6th September

Today was the first day back at school, and I have so much to say.

And it is all about one person-Dakota.

The first chance I got to see her was in History. Which was my first lesson after form. She is like a different person. Her hair is insane. It used to be a wild, brown mess full of curls- now it's completely straight with thick bright red streaks going down to the ends like those Japanese girls in Manga. Everyone was talking about it. No one could believe it was the same person. It wasn't just her hair, though. Her skin was tanned golden brown, and she was wearing makeup, subtle and classy, like lip-gloss and stuff. As far as I knew she never wore any before, except at weddings, and family parties. Her ears looked good, too. The new piercings looked fresh and completely epic.

No one noticed my hair. My mum straightened it this morning, to show it off the layers like before and I felt good about it. I thought people would see I did something with it, and it looked nice. I never bothered with haircuts before. This was the first time I ever had it styled in any way.

When I saw Dakota at break and lunchtime, she said she had taken up surfing and had been doing it all summer. Her mum got her a pair of GHDs for her birthday. Dakota looked great. It was strange, though, because she looked completely different. She still looked like Dakota but maybe not so much my Dakota. I didn't know how I felt about it. I was in awe of her. I studied her, trying to take it all in. Her green eyes popped with the makeup she had on. I wonder how she found out to do it. Apply it, so it enhanced her features but still looked natural. Her hair felt so soft; Dakota let me touch it. I asked if she wanted to feel mine, but she said, "that's okay."

Dakota said, "If I want to keep the streaks, I have to keep getting them redone so they stay bright red."

"You should totally keep them," I said.

She smiled and said, "I think so too."

I told Dakota she looked as pretty as Anne, the trapeze artist in The Greatest Showman.

I love her ears. Dakota told me she eventually wants a string of them at the top of each one. Mum won't let me have my ears done, even the normal lobe bit. Dad is adamant I have to be 16. I wish my parents were more like Dakota's. Mine live in the dark ages. I can't even get a job. It wasn't until the end of lunchtime that Dakota asked me about my 'blip' and if I was okay. I said I didn't want to talk about it. I made sure she hadn't told anyone.

Dakota promised me she hadn't, not even her mum or her sister, Ellie. So, I said, "Good, keep it between us."

She didn't know what to say apart from "Okay."

Dakota was a bit off with me all day. I know she thinks I'm a mess. She probably looked at my hair and assumed I was trying to copy her with a new look. Steal her thunder or something.

She seemed really distant. We didn't laugh and joke like we usually did. Instead, Dakota kept looking at other people, like a group of the more popular kids like Johanna Robinson and Tucker Greenway. We used to make fun of them all the time, about how they care about dumb stuff like selfies for Instagram and eating zero calories. But when I made a joke, Dakota didn't react or join in.

My first day back was pretty tedious. The only thing I got out of it was the cold shoulder from Dakota and a whack of homework I didn't want. I hope tomorrow is a better day.

Dakota has a boyfriend! She told me this morning. As far as I know, she hasn't gone out with anyone before, so it was a bit of a shock! Three weeks together already, apparently. But the biggest surprise was when I found out who it was. Jamie Parsons!!!!!

Jamie was this little kid, a total nerd, all geeky, short, and skinny. He looked about 8 even though he was the same age as us. He always hung round with Luca Young, despite the fact Luca was a popular kid and Jamie was a total dweeb. They had been friends since nursery and known each other forever. I asked Dakota if she was sure, it was the same boy, but she said he changed quite a bit over the summer. I thought she was kidding, but then I saw him. Jamie must have got a few growth spurts because he was really tall. His hair was still blonde but it's beachier now, and he looked quite a bit older, like he got made over or something. Dakota said they bumped into each other at the ear-piercing place; he was having the same thing done as her. He told her he always liked her, even with all the frizzy hair but thought she was into more edgy guys with nail varnish. Jamie surfs, too; they've been hanging out together for ages. Which explains why his skin was also really brown.

When Dakota talked about him, she was all smiley, like she was telling a funny story. I guess she really likes him. Jamie's even met BB, her dog, short for Bumblebee. They've taken him out for walks and that.

I am glad she's happy, but I'm also quite angry. While I was home alone, Dakota was with Jamie. Although we are meant to be best friends, I'm unsure if she wants to be with me anymore.

Worse still, I had PE today. I hate PE. The other girls all stare and judge me when I get undressed in front of them. I'm all skinny and pale, with these giant boobs that don't fit in with the rest of me. I keep my hair long to cover them, but it's no good. I have spots all over my body in places they shouldn't. I always get odd ones on my back, top of my chest, behind my neck, even on my bum. I know I should be grateful they aren't littered all over my body head to toe, like Jenna Walker and Dominic Green, but why do they exist? What is the purpose of spots? They are torture! Sometimes, they are sore, and you feel them through your clothes. I can't stand pus. When I get spots, if I can see the pus, I squeeze as quickly as I can to get it all out. Mum said you should leave them and put ice on them, but who can cope with white boulders all over your face?

Between you and me, it's pretty satisfying seeing the pus pop out, although it's also a bit gross. Sometimes it bleeds, which means you have to keep dabbing tissue and check a little river of blood isn't beginning to run down your face. Before you realise it, the blood dries up and you look like an extra from a horror movie. Just before they bleed, they get all red, incredibly bright like a beacon, and it is the only thing noticeable on your entire face. Spots are absolutely horrific!

I knew a boy once who went over a spot with a razor. He put a plaster on it and said he cut himself shaving. I don't know if he did it on purpose. This was in year 8. Girls can't do that. The ones on your face are the worst because they can't be covered up. I have a massive red bump on my chin right now. I hate it.

Dakota and I sat on the playground bench, and she suddenly got up and left with Jamie and Luca. He called her over, and she said, "Coming!" Only as an afterthought did she ask me if I wanted to come. Why would I want to go with her, her boyfriend and Luca? I don't know them. She'd be all loved up, and I'd be stuck with Luca Young, with who I have zero in common. So, I sat there. On the bench alone while she went off with her new friends, I was left abandoned staring at the floor.

I don't know how long I was there before it happened, but a girl came and sat next to me. I didn't hear or see anyone come and sit down. I have never seen anyone like her. She had dark hair and a thick streak of bright blue on the side facing me. She sat with her head down; I heard rock music through her headphones. I couldn't tell what she was listening to, but I knew it was one of those cool unknown bands you had to be like a true music fan to know about.

I think she must be new or recently moved schools because I didn't recognise her, and I was desperate to see her face. She was wearing the school skirt, and I noticed it rested high on her leg. The girl was petite and must be athletic as she was slim and nicely toned.

I looked up, and I saw she was staring right at me. She had the most beautiful face I have ever seen and piercings on her nose and bottom lip. She had these huge, big green eyes like Dakota's. So pretty and cool. I realised she must have seen me looking at her. She was staring at the spot on my chin with pure disgust. I tried to smile to invite conversation, but she got up and said, "Loser." The girl walked away.

When I got home after school, I went straight upstairs without speaking to Mum or Mac. Mum followed me up and knocked on my door. When I gave her the okay, she opened it and came inside.

"What's wrong?"

I couldn't answer her, so I stayed silent. I didn't know how to say I was caught looking at a girl who now thought I was a repulsive pervert. Or that I was attracted to her and didn't know what this meant. Or that I lost my only friend to a boy.

After an uncomfortable silence, Mum tried another tack. "Have you been writing in the book I gave you?"

"Yes."

She sat at the end of my bed. "Can you tell me just one thing that happened today?"

"Dakota has a boyfriend. Except it's not really Dakota. It's like this made-over version with straight hair, red streaks, a tan, and piercings. She's now with Jamie, who spent all summer on the beach with her and her dog. He used to be a real dweeb who looked tiny, but he's all different now too. Jamie's like a boy band surfer guy now

and pretty tall. They are really into each other, and I don't know what to do about it."

"It's still Dakota. She's still your best friend. You guys are growing up, that's all. Things will keep changing because you are becoming adults and who you are meant to be."

Mum moved toward where I was lying on the bed and put her arm around me in a cuddle. "Does Dakota really like this boy? Jamie?"

"Don't know, maybe. I'm not sure if she's even had a boyfriend before."

"Really? That's surprising. Dakota's such a pretty girl."

This made me wonder if Mum thinks I am pretty. I know she's got to say yes, or she's a lousy parent. But if there was no maternal obligation, would Mum, hand on her heart, say I was a pretty girl? I don't think she would. My hair, for starters, it's so long and thin, not thick like Dakota's.

Dakota looks incredible. People were amazed by her on Monday; she took their breath away. They really noticed her. I wish I had that, for one day. Even for an hour. No wonder she has a boyfriend. Boys don't like me; I don't feel anything toward them either. I see some as attractive, sure. But I feel that way toward girls too. I don't know if that means there's something wrong with me. I'm not into girly things; I don't wear dresses or makeup or feel inclined to. I don't go shopping, giggle, or wear bikinis. I like hoodies, films, and drawing.

Am I gay? Bi? Asexual? I felt drawn toward that girl today. I stare at Dakota. Do I like girls? If I keep looking, does that mean I fancy her? Everyone seems to know what they are. I am so confused.

I know it sounds weird, but I miss her. The way Dakota was before she changed. It feels like everything is changing, and I can't keep up. Where do I fit in?

Mum said we're growing up and changing, but into what? When will I know what I want to be? Who I am? When will I know who I want to be? Does Dakota know? Is that why she's so different? When will that happen to me?

Mum stroked my hair. It felt nice. "Dakota is your best friend. You owe it to all those years of friendship to try and hang out with her and her boyfriend. You might be pleasantly surprised, and he could become a new friend."

I am sure every parent thinks teenage friendships are something straight out of a cheesy movie where everyone gets along, and we all break into song across the playground.

"If you care about her," Mum continued. "You should give him a chance."

I do care about Dakota.

"Okay," I said. "I'll make an effort."

Friday

This morning has not gone well.

I had vision problems first thing, followed by pains in my chest. After that, I found breathing hard, making me feel dizzy and lightheaded. My heart was pumping like crazy through my chest; I couldn't slow it down. It felt like it was going to burst through my school shirt. I banged my hairbrush hard against the door as I couldn't speak. Mum and Mac came rushing into my room.

It felt like I was going to die. My body was giving up. Severe pains in my chest, I was petrified it was a heart attack.

I looked despairingly at Mum and Mac to save me.

"Augusta, you're okay. I promise you are okay."

I'm going to die. I can't breathe.

"Ambulance," I managed to whisper.

Mum held my hands together in hers. "No, darling, you don't need an ambulance. This has happened before, and you were okay, remember?"

I could feel Mac's hand rubbing my back. "Your body is full of adrenalin. It will settle. Just try and breathe." My chest was being pushed through my body. My throat closed in, and my body was on fire.

"I know it feels like you have no control. This is normal. The adrenalin will settle. Remember before," Mac went on. "You are fine, this is normal, you are okay, trust me, it will pass. Nothing bad is going to happen to you."

All I could think was I am so afraid.

"Your body will exhaust itself; it will settle." Mum put her forehead to mine, forcing me to focus on her. "Oh baby, you're sweating buckets. You will be okay, remember before. You came out okay."

"Breathe, Augusta. Breathe." I concentrated on hearing Mac's words.

"Breathe, Augusta. Breathe." He sounded so calm.

"Breathe. You can do this. Just breathe." I put all my efforts into breathing deep and slowly out.

"That's it. Keep going. Breathe."

My breathing slowed. I looked around as if I was seeing my bedroom for the first time. Dazed, lightheaded and disorientated. I felt groggy and unsteady, but I knew I was going to be alright.

"You're okay," Mum said as she hugged me. "You're okay."

"I'll put the shower on for you," Mac said as he left my room.
He came back with a bottle of water. "Here, drink this."
It was nice and cold. I drank it all, had a shower and heard Mum talking to the school. I wasn't going in. My body felt exhausted. Mum rang the hospital; said she wasn't coming in today and arranged to cover or move all her appointments.

I spent the rest of the day watching Back to the Future Movies and the Greatest Showman with Mum cuddled on the sofa.

I drew this in my notebook while watching Back to the Future part 2. I showed my Mum, she really liked it.

Today was the first time I saw Dakota at a time other than in class. When we sat in French, she apologised to me.

"I shouldn't have left you the other day. Sorry, mate." I told her it was okay.

"You know they really aren't that bad," she continued, "I'm meeting up with them at lunchtime; why don't you come along? Get to know everyone a bit better. I know J wants to get to know you."

"J?"

"Sorry, Jamie. We call each other J and D- it's just easier."

"Okay."

I was nervous and fidgety throughout Dual-Science and watched the clock like a countdown. Dakota sat next to me even though Jamie was also in our class, which was nice.

We were looking at plant cells through microscopes, which was quite interesting. Most leaves look the same, but when you look closer, they aren't perfect or symmetrical. They're a bit like paving, but all misshapen and different sizes. Every bit is unique. From far away, leaves look pristine and ordinary, even perfect, but they are all flawed and inexact. Each leaf has its own chaos hidden away.

It's deceptive. Everyone walks by hundreds of leaves every day. They look so well put together, but it's an illusion. The world doesn't look twice. They assume each leaf is the same as all the others on the branch or stem.

Yet they are chaotic, random, confused, erratic and complex, but somehow, they hold it all together. You must look closely beneath the surface to discover what's inside. Only then can you find out the mess within. Every leaf is doing the same thing. Holding it all in, concealing its own little patchwork of mayhem. They all hide it so well that no one even notices. It made me quite emotional the more I thought about it. Leaves are alive. How can we be sure they don't feel pain even if they don't have the brains to register what pain is. They may feel alone, cold, and forgotten when they drop. Is that their equivalent of a 'blip'? Their downfall?

The bell rang.

Dakota gave me a gentle nudge. "Ready?"

I was not. But I gave a half smile anyway.

We saw Jamie outside the classroom. He was chatting with Drew Abbottson, so he said he'd catch up with us outside by the bench.

We went to the playground. It wasn't long before Jamie, and his cronies came over. Dakota sat beside me moving her foot up and down annoyingly, but she perked up as soon as she saw him. She looked happy. I looked at Jamie, and so did he. They were both acting like it was Christmas or their birthday or something. Silly, really, they only just saw each other in science.

"Hey, D."

"Hi, J."

I don't think they realise how stupid that sounds.

"You want to come and hang out near the trees, under the shade? You too, Augusta."

Jamie's voice is quite deep and more profound than I thought. Johanna Robinson, the school bitch already looked pissed off standing behind Luca Young. She had her arms folded and a sulky look on her face. So did her little gang members Tamara and Renee. All their school skirts were shortened till they barely covered their bum. Their hair was all straight like Dakota's, but their make-up was less subtle. Johanna, Tamara, and Renee went everywhere together.

Rosie, a girl in a few of my classes, stepped toward me. "Hey Augusta, right? I'm Rosie. I think you're in my Art class. Your stuff is brilliant."

I stepped closer to her and said I liked her stuff too. After that, everyone walked toward the clearing near the back of the school. It was really sunny and had a lot of trees, so it was a bit cooler.

Rosie's nice. She is going out with Luca, Jamie's best friend. They have been since they were about 12. At this point, Dakota moved closer to Jamie, they were holding hands and looking at each other.

Rosie chatted about art quite a bit. She said she liked the idea of becoming an artist for a living, but it would be so hard-going, and most artists barely earn enough to get by, so it wasn't overly practical or realistic. But she loves the idea of 'struggling for your art'.

Johanna and her gang of imitators were obviously eavesdropping on our conversation.

"Why choose to struggle? It makes no sense," Johanna piped in. "Honestly, Rosie, you don't half talk a lot of crap sometimes."

Luca tried to stick up for Rosie, but what was remarkable was Rosie didn't need him- she stuck up for herself. "Because you would paint from the heart, your work would mean something. Your life would be full of passion, and you would leave behind a bit of your soul to the world, not live a superficial, meaningless existence which you would regret by the time you hit 50."

Either it was too deep for Johanna, or she didn't care. "Well, I think it sounds like a load of crap."

Predictably the two copycats beside her agreed. My mum always taught me that even if you are bottom of the class but willing to listen and ready to learn, you are never the dumbest. The highest form of ignorance is when you presume something, close your mind off and fail to listen to others to consider their view. I thought about that when Johanna kept talking crap. I would have told Rosie about it if we were alone or if Johanna, Renee, and Tamara weren't there. I think she would have liked it.

We finally came to the trees Jamie had been talking about. The shade was vital as the sun was blinding. I was actually feeling okay. Rosie was friendly, Luca and Jamie seemed OK, and Dakota was with me. She kept looking over at me and smiling, making sure I smiled back to let her know I was alright. And I was genuinely okay. Tucker Greenway and Zayn Lancaster were also there.
I sat on the grass next to Rosie and Luca. Johanna was laughing and showing Tucker and Tamara pictures guys had sent her on her phone. They were all laughing at them. I wondered if the guys who sent them to Johanna knew she'd be mocking them and showing people. It was obviously pictures of their private parts, judging by the comments. Tucker grabbed Johanna's phone, which annoyed her, she swore and called him a ass.

Tucker brought the phone over to us. "What do you think of that, Augusta? Huh? Anything familiar?" He was finding it hysterical.

I didn't look. I kept moving my head so I wouldn't see.

"Tucker, get it away," Rosie told him, sounding slightly exasperated.

Tucker moved the phone toward Rosie's face. "What about you, Rosie? How does my boy, Luca, here compare? Huh?"

Rosie pushed him away, clearly irritated. "Ew."

"Tucker, get it out of here!" Luca ordered. Thankfully Tucker finally got the message and ran back to Johanna, laughing.

Luca apologised to me. I told him it was okay.

I looked back to Johanna. She, Tamara, and Renee were taking selfies, hitching their skirts up on one side and undoing shirt buttons showing glimpses of their underwear.

"I'm going to get a drink," I said. The sun was hot, even in the shade. I could feel myself sweating already and felt so thirsty.

To my horror, Johanna stopped posing and said, "We'll come with you."

Panic.

I tried to say, "That's alright", but it came out in a whisper. In hope, I looked over at Dakota, but she was cuddling Jamie, and they were looking and smiling at each other. As a reserve, I sought out Rosie, but she was busy kissing Luca. As a result, I was on my own.

Tucker suddenly called over, "I'll come too. I fancy something sweet." And he winked at Renee, who giggled. "Yeah, you know what I mean." He continued smiling widely.

Johanna called him a pig, so he made pig noises and got on his hands and knees, snorting and crawling on the grass. It was pretty funny. He looked over at me and seemed to like I was laughing. He leered at me, "Oh, you like that? I bet you do, you dirty girl."

I didn't know what to do.

"Tucker! Leave her alone!" Jamie called over.

"Hey, Zayn!" Tucker shouted. "Going canteen, are you coming?"

Zayn Lancaster gave a thumbs up and joined us. Lots of girls in our school fancy him. He is really sporty and has hair that flops down over his eyes. Zayn's the kind of guy everyone likes but is always in the distance. You could never imagine being close to him unless you are one of the privileged few. He was out of everyone's league. I couldn't believe how close I was to him now.

 Zayn caught up and slapped both hands on Tuckers' shoulders. "Sorry about him, we are all really nice. Honest." And he gave me this amazing smile.

Zayn Lancaster actually smiled at me. It felt so surreal.

He linked arms with Tucker and me and we started walking. "Come on, I fancy a Snickers."

After a moment or two, he let go, and we all walked casually along the path. He enquired what I was doing next and if I had anything going on at the weekend. Zayn Lancaster was asking me about my plans! I couldn't believe it!

We got to the canteen, I bought some water, and the rest of the group got their stuff. The boys played some tag game down the corridor, and I was left with Johanna, Tamara, and Renee.

Johanna turned to me and said, "it's so different having someone like you in our group."

I responded with, "someone like me?"

"You know, such a work in progress. But like, obviously, without any progress."

"Oh my God, so much!" Tamara chirped in straight after.

I have often wondered if Tamara has ever had an original thought or idea that didn't centre around Johanna's.

Renee squealed. "I just had a brilliant idea!" She let out a little scream and waved her hands around. "We. Should. Do. A. Makeover." She paused after every word as if anything Renee had to say was of any importance.

My neck felt all tight and smothered, and I found it hard to take a breath.

They all laughed as if it was the funniest thing in the world. I, Augusta Walsh, was the funniest thing in the world. They were laughing at me.

"How much money do you think I have, Renee!?!" Johanna spurted between her manipulative, evil nasty cackling. "I'd be bankrupt! I mean, look at her!" I concentrated so hard on trying not to react. I still had trouble breathing in and out. But there was nothing I could do. The tears were coming. I yawned to try and give some kind of plausible explanation for why my eyes were watering. I hated myself. My whole face felt hot, and I rubbed my eyes hard. They were now stinging as the tears ran down my face. I tried to be silent and brush them away as quickly as they came, but they were falling fast now. Instead, I did the worst thing. As I breathed in, I made that sound you only make when you are full-on blubbering.

They were too busy mocking me to notice at first, but Johanna paused and said, "I'm sorry, but you know..." she looked at me. "Oh my God, are you crying?"

"She is!" Tamara screamed in vicious, hateful, sadistic glee, and like a gang of witches, they wickedly laughed again.

The tears flowed faster. I couldn't keep up, so I did the only thing I could. I ran to the toilet. The nearest one was at the end of the corridor. I almost crashed into Tucker and Zayn as I raced by. They both yelled after me.

I could feel my heart about to explode through my chest. I kept my head down as I heard the girls' cruelty follow me. Finally, I bolted through the toilet door and headed straight into the nearest cubicle. I sat on the toilet and sobbed. The bathroom was echoey, but I could hear whispering and a door open or close.

Unfortunately for me, there was no loo roll, so I had to use the sleeve of my jumper. Afterwards, I realised I didn't have my bottle of water. I must have dropped it in my rush to get in here and escape their ridicule.

I thought about what I had that afternoon, English Lit and Lang. None of that group would be there. When there was no more crying to betray me, I slowly splashed water on my face and opened the toilet door. There was no one there. I kept my head down and got to class.

When I came home, I went straight upstairs and wrote inside you. I am relying on this book more to say stuff I can't tell anyone else. I don't know why I am the way I am. I don't want to be this snivelling fool and loser. But I don't know what to do or how I can fix it and make myself like everyone else.

The only thing or person I can relate to is a leaf.

Mac was really nice to me tonight. After I got into my onesie after school, I came downstairs to make some toast.

Mac was making a coffee. "Hey kiddo, Woah...serious onesie. Tough day at school?"

"A little."

"Your Mum's at work doing visits for a bit. So why don't you lay on the sofa for a bit, and I'll bring you something?"

I nodded, grabbed the TV remote, and lay down on the sofa. A little bit later, Mac came through with a tray. It had my favourite meal- nachos with all the trimmings. Peppers, tomatoes, tons of cheese, garlic mayo- the lot 😊 . Beside it was a bowl of ice cream, a little ramekin of jellybeans, and a can of diet coke.

I smiled; it was what I needed. "Thanks, Mac."

He gave me a massive smile back like I did him a huge favour, leant down and kissed me on the forehead. "If you need me, I'll be in the office."

I thanked him again and popped on some Netflix to watch a few episodes of The Big Bang Theory.

Mum got home at teatime and asked if I needed to talk. I told her no. There's nothing she could do. We tried watching a film after we ate, but I couldn't concentrate as I was worried about what would happen in school tomorrow.

What annoys me most about Johanna Robinson is how much power she seems to have. How is she so popular, get to do what she likes, yet acts so entitled and a total shrew to everyone? People think she's the best thing ever. Even some of the teachers are up her ass. She looks fake. Teeth whitened, extended hair, her family are wealthy and paid to make her into this plastic-looking monster. All I see when I look at her is an ugly mess. She always has lots of

make-up, wears heels to school, and has zero personality because she's always putting on an act. The school seems to let her bend the rules constantly. It's not fair.

Tamara copies her completely. She dyed her hair, so it's the same colour and wears it the same way. Her family have less money, though. Tamara has crooked teeth but refuses to have braces on the NHS. She copies Johanna's style, too, a complete sheep.

I wish things were different. I don't want to have to clone others so I can fit in. I want to be real, not hated for it. When will that time be? I wish I had the confidence or a big, thick narcissistic streak, so I didn't care and did what I wanted. When will everyone be able to genuinely be themselves and feel free? I want to have the courage not to hide away from who I am, to speak out about my thoughts and views without fear or judgement and show the world the person I am deep inside. Reveal every layer, but I know they would laugh and decide I am a worthless, ignorant, untalented, lost cause that no one wants to know.

I went upstairs halfway through the film and scrolled through TikTok and Instagram. I found Zayn's Insta profile, but it was private. He had over 3,280 followers! How does he know so many people? I am on Instagram, but not really. I don't post anything. On TikTok, I have a profile, but I only do videos of me drawing stuff. People seem to like it. But I don't have as many followers as Zayn. Most of the people who follow me on TikTok I have never met. I only meant to go on for 20 minutes, but it was well past midnight when I stopped looking through it all.

It's been a couple of days since I've written, but I have massive news!

Dakota came up after that day and asked if I was okay and why I ran off without telling her or saying goodbye?

I told her I was just bored. She was a bit annoyed. She asked if I wanted to come to hang out again, but I said, "no."

I don't want to see Johanna more than I absolutely have to. I don't understand why she likes it so much. I know she wants to be with her boyfriend, but it's Jamie Parsons, not Harry Styles!

I told her, "I don't want to hang out with them anymore."

Dakota said, "thanks for trying", in a really bitchy tone.

"I did try Dakota. And yeah, Rosie and Zayn weren't too bad, and Jamie and Luca were alright, but the rest of them aren't my sort of people."

"I gotta go." And she got up and left. So, I watched her go, and the next thing I knew, that girl was there again. The pretty one with piercings who listens to cool rock music. Her hair was up, and I saw she had her ears pierced at the top, same as Dakotas.

"Not a great friend, are you?" she said, looking in the direction Dakota walked away.

I didn't answer her. I didn't know what to say.

The girl turned to me, "she's probably outgrown you anyway. Moved on."

I kept quiet; it was like the girl was seeing inside my mind. We sat quietly.

Her phone rang, breaking the silence. She took out her mobile; I knew it was an iPhone. I always wanted one, but my mum could only afford a no-brand android on contract. It was still a smartphone, thank goodness. But I wouldn't mind something a bit better.

"Yeah?" She was obviously too important to say hello. Too boring for her.

"Tonight? Sounds cool." Of course, she gets invited out.

"Meet at the pub? Nah, don't worry, I got one.
Yeah, I might play a little. Cool, see you then." I had so many questions.

The whole time I watched her tongue intently, the way it moved. I have never been so fascinated with another person. It makes sense she would be daring enough to go to a pub. I look too young; I wouldn't get served. I wanted to ask her questions- what was she doing? What did she play? I wished I could know how to ask to go with her or see her there. Would it be wrong to ask her if I could come?

Straight after, her conversation ended, she made a call.

"Hi Mum, it's Thai. I'm going out tonight to the pub with a few friends. Is that, ok? Cheers, bye."

I couldn't believe how easy it was for her. But the massive bit of information I got from it was her name. Thai. Such a cool name! I wish I had a name like that.

She put her headphones in, looked at me, said, "see ya," and walked away.

Today, I had Drama. I hate Drama. I only took it because Dakota went on about choosing it, and I wanted to be with her. It turned out to be for nothing as her sister, Ellie, told her Media Studies would be a far more enjoyable subject to study. I was torn between Drama and Photography as I had been getting good grades in both. A couple of years ago, I could act. For every play, it was always a toss-up between me and Chloe for the main supporting part. I hate speaking out now. It is embarrassing- I get sweaty, my leg shakes, and my voice wobbles. Everything I say is stupid.

In class, we divided into groups and had to create a scene where two opposite people in personalities try to mix together in a typical daily scenario like a café etc. The teacher gave the café as an example, so of course, pretty much every group did a café. I was with Jennifer and Chloe. Both are nice to me and are leading performers and organisers of stuff in the school. They get good grades, and lots of teachers like them a lot.

In Drama, we are studying Blood Brothers, which is about two boys- twins- who are separated at birth and brought up in different areas of the city, so the whole exercise counted toward that.

Jennifer is loud, and I'm pretty quiet, so we thought Chloe could help us improvise, moving the conversation along. I like being with Jennifer and Chloe as they do a lot of work and always have lots of ideas.

Our teacher, Mrs Kenyon, called us together so we could see everyone's scenes. Jennifer is a complete extrovert. She's pretty out there and draws quite a lot of attention to herself. It was quite hard standing up there with her as everyone was watching us, and Johanna, Tamara and Rosie are all in my Drama class too.

Johanna and Tamara were pointing and laughing at us. I didn't like all the attention. Jennifer seemed to feed upon it and continued to get louder and louder.

I tried my best and did what we set out to do. My part was to order a drink and a meal and sit in the corner. Jennifer was singing, dancing, and complaining her coffee was cold. I didn't think we did a good job, all the time I tried not to look at Johanna. But when I did briefly, I saw Thai sitting next to her, which threw me a bit.

Thai shouted over, "You're doing everything wrong! You have no idea what you are doing, Augusta!" She was laughing at me.

I felt myself well up and tried to hold it in. I continued the scene with my head down and body slumped over to hide my face. Finally, our turn was over. It was only meant to last 5 minutes; I'm sure we did more like 20. I sat on the floor next to Chloe and kept my head down, so my hair hung over my face.

Johanna, Tamara, and Rosie also did a café, but someone beautiful and ugly. The teacher told them looks were not personality traits. Mrs Kenyon, our Drama teacher, values students who do the work, not just popular ones in the school. For this reason, I like her a lot.

When I looked up, Thai was gone.

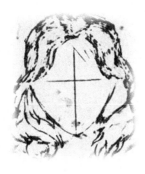

Amazingly, I saw her again though later in PHSE. I had never seen her there before. I couldn't believe it, three times in one day. My teacher, Mr Davies, began to talk about gender and sexuality. He asked us, "Who doesn't identify as a gender?" Half raised their hand. Thai was in front with her back to me. I sat on my own, a few tables back as Dakota was next to Jamie. Neither of them put their hand up, and I couldn't see if Thai had either.

Mr Davies went on a bit; I wasn't listening. I was too busy trying to look at Thai. It was a bit like a concert when your view is blocked, and you're trying to see the main attraction. I could see the top of her head and half of her face. He asked about sexuality. Mr Davies said, "only share if you feel comfortable, " it was "a safe place".

Mr Davies is actually dumb when it comes to what kids are actually like in our school. They are mean and nasty, nowhere is safe.

When he asked if any of us ever had feelings for another girl or boy. Again, I did not put my hand up. I couldn't see if Thai did either, but a few did.

"See?" said Mr Davies with a hint of triumph, "you are not alone."

Obviously, feeling like he had gained our trust and we were under the 'safe place' illusion, he decided to try his luck. "Okay, let's ask another question. I admit it's a little more difficult. But remember, we are all friends here." Good grief.

"Has anyone ever felt bi-curious?"

I tried not to react and sunk a little in my chair. At that moment, Tommy Waterman dropped his pen on the floor and bent down to pick it up. I had a crystal-clear view of her and there was no mistaking it.

Thai's hand was in the air.

I spent last night at Dad's place. I don't enjoy staying there very much. I tend to get away with one weekend every three weeks. I blame it on school homework and stress. My parents agreed to it after my 'blip'. Before then, it was once a fortnight.

Of course, I love him, but he's a bit boring. Dad doesn't do very much or take me anywhere. He's always too depressed to cook, so we have the same microwave meals as he doesn't know what else to feed me. His place is tiny, but Dad does keep it neat and clean. But he also never knows what to say, so we both end up underwhelmed. Dad drinks quite a bit whenever I stay over, there's always a bottle of Bells whiskey on the table, and it's guaranteed to be almost empty in the morning when I leave. Dad always apologises to me for not being better, for giving me a rubbish time, and how he'll be better next visit. He also says maybe we'll go bowling, ice skating, or to the cinema, but we never do. I wish he would try, but I guess I'm not exactly a ball of fun to hang around with. Usually, I count down the hours till I can go home again. At his place, all I do is draw or play on my phone. Dad sits there, watches TV and plays on his phone opposite me.

I never tell Dad what a terrible time I'm having because I don't want to hurt his feelings. But he makes me want to scream, DO SOMETHING WITH ME!!! STOP IGNORING ME!!! TAKE ME OUT!!!!

I know he hasn't got much money, but we can go to the beach or take a walk. I even offered to pay for us to go to the cinema so he wouldn't feel pressured to talk to me. Dad said, "No."

He never used to be like this; Dad used to get home from work and be so excited to see us- he always said the highlight of his day was coming home. If the sun was shining, Dad would tell us to put our shoes on, exclaiming 'the day was too good to waste'. It would drive him insane being cooped up in an office all day when he could have been outside. When I was younger, I loved fairies and unicorns, and Dad would find all these fairy trails for us to go on.

For my 10th birthday, I woke up to an invitation, all gold embossed, to a magical gathering in the wood. There was even a gold map, Mum looked at it, memorised the directions and we got in the car. I asked where my dad was,

 and Mum said he would see me in a little while after he sorted my birthday cake. "So," she said, "we have to take lots of pictures as I'm sure he would love to be here and watch you go on this adventure."

So, she drove us as I followed our location with my finger on the map in the back seat. When we got there, it was a big forest. A sign was beside a gate with my name and an arrow. We set off down the path. Lanterns hung from the trees, and at the bottom of the trunks were little doors beside tiny washing lines with miniature dresses. Along the path were small houses with minuscule furniture and pocket offerings with my name. Tags inscribed with 'the honorary fairy Augusta' scrolled in gold lettering. I collected a tiara, wings, a flower bracelet, a butterfly ring, and a large silver key. It was magical, and I felt so special. Folded notes were dotted about under the arms of little teddy bears, saying *you're beautiful* and *follow your dreams.*

Holding Mum's hand, the trail led to a clearing. There was Dad, stroking a white horse bearing a white unicorn horn and plaited mane. Along with a real-life Tinkerbell who sang as we came into view.

I gazed in wonder, then I ran and hugged the horse. I wrapped my arms around Dad, who was crying, tears streaming, and I asked if I had done something wrong. But he said, "No, good tears. Happy birthday, sweetheart!" He lifted me up, swung me round, and sat me down onto the unicorn. Tinkerbell took the reins, and we went for a ride. When I returned, she gave me a special gift: a silver charm bracelet. My friends from school appeared wearing fairy and elves costumes. It was an incredible day. My favourite birthday I ever had.

I asked Mum about this day a couple years ago, and she told me it was all Dad. Apart from inviting my friends, he did the whole thing. Organised it all from the embossed invitation to the unicorn, keepsakes, and trail of little houses.

I guess loving me was a lot easier back then. I'm not even sure if he likes me now.

I AM NO LONGER FRIENDS WITH DAKOTA. I asked her out straight, "What exactly did I do, Dakota? Why aren't we hanging out anymore?"

She told me, "I'm always hanging out with you! I'm with you all the time! What more do you want!?!"
But that's a lie. We used to hang out after school, but we haven't done that for ages. I loved us watching films together like The Greatest Showman or hanging out people-watching on benches in town, eating pizza and drinking cokes.

That's not the only thing she lied about. I asked her if she knew anything about Thai since she's friends with Johanna and her wannabes, but Dakota kept pretending she didn't know who I was talking about!

It got me a bit frustrated. "The girl in PHSE, with all the piercings, the streak of blue hair? She's sat one table across from you! How could you not see her? THAI!"

"I never saw any girl called Thai; you know I never pay attention in PHSE! It's such a bogus subject. What's her last name? Maybe it'll ring a bell."

I looked down and mumbled, "I don't know it."
Dakota shrugged, "okay."

"Can you ask Johanna if she knows her?"

"No, I hardly speak to Johanna," she lied. "And I haven't seen this Thai, so I can't even describe her properly."

I felt increasingly angry at her; she wasn't even willing to try. I asked Dakota if she could come over to mine after school today, but she said she was "seeing J". Always Jamie! Literally going off with him all the time. It's so annoying! I want things back to how they were before they got together.

I was still looking at the floor, but Dakota tilted her head and made her face my entire view. Her hair hung down, and the sunlight from behind illuminated the red streaks. She looked like an angel. I couldn't help but smile at her, only vaguely aware of what she was saying. I asked her to repeat it.

"I said, come over to the café this Saturday. I can give you a free coke and ice cream?"

Dakota works at this Café on Saturdays as a waitress. But there's the thing, she HAS to be there. That's not making time for us, is it? I can't keep putting in all the effort, chasing after her like a lapdog. It's a joke.

I told her I'd think about it, but I wish we could hang out properly. We are meant to be best friends, after all. I've not seen her all summer; she seems to be all about Jamie or 'J' now; I'm not sure where I fit in. He's okay, but I want it to be the two of us, not the three of us. At the moment, I have to hang out with Tucker and the rest of them every time I want to see her. It's not fair!

In Ethics this afternoon, I got to class early and sat next to Chloe when Mark Weston walked in with Jeffrey Thomas. They dropped condoms on Jennifer's desk; some fell on her lap, where she sat next to Meredith, her best mate.

"Here you go, Jenny, you dirty strumpet."

"Nice bit of prep for next time," Jeffrey piped in. "Better safe than sorry."

They thought this was hilarious, and other boys high-fived them as they sat down near the back. I wasn't too sure what was going on.

Our Ethics teacher, Mr Wallis, was unloading his satchel, he told them to come to pick up their rubbish.

I looked at Jennifer. Her face was bright red. I have never known her to be so quiet. Jennifer is always the first to talk and take centre stage in Drama. It made me feel uneasy seeing her so sombre and downcast. Something wasn't right.

I whispered to Chloe and asked her, "What's going on?"

"Dominic Green told everyone he and Jennifer slept together, and now it's all over the school."
Is it true?" I couldn't imagine them together at all. Dominic is small for his age. In fact, people often think he's in the years below because he is so tiny. Plus, he has acne all over his face and body, not exactly lover material. Jennifer's no oil painting, but she is pretty in her own way and can do better.

"No, Augusta, of course not! Jen told me boys were teasing him, calling him a virgin. They only came out of science about 10 minutes before, so she was the first girl he thought of as they always sat together. He completely threw her under the bus. "

"But why would he do that?"

"Why do boys do anything? The jerk even said they did it three times- once in the library and twice in his dad's car. Jen has never even met his dad or seen Dominic outside of school! But of course, people believe the creep, Jen is being called a slut, and no one will stop talking about it."
The boys were still noisy and cheering each other on, so Mr Wallis spoke to them again. "Come and pick these up, please, and settle down at the back."

Mark Weston stood up, and Mr Wallis picked up the condoms and held them out for him to collect.

Jennifer's head was down. Jeffrey Thomas shouted as he came to the front, "Got a bit of a sweet spot for her, have we, Sir? She been shagging you too?"

Mr Wallis's whole face changed and went red as he roared, "GET OUT OF MY CLASS NOW, YOU DESPICABLE BOY!" he gave Jeffrey detention as he passed him. Walking out, Jeffrey was saying, "whatever."

Meredith stood up, "Jeffrey, you're an idiot! Jen's no slapper; Dominic is lying!"

Mr Wallis told Meredith to sit down. As Mark Weston came to collect the condoms from Mr Wallis, Jennifer flinched as he came near her. I think Mr Wallis noticed.

"You too, Mark, please!" he called. Mark Weston, who was back in his chair, stood up, grabbed his bag, and shuffled out.

I looked at Jennifer. Her hands were over her stomach, and Meredith had her arm around her, whispering.

"Are you alright, Jen?" Chloe asked her.

Jennifer silently nodded and leaned back in her seat.

In French, Dakota told me she spoke to her mum and would make more time for me. She said, "you are my best friend. No one can take your place, not even J." Which I thought was quite sweet.

"Thanks, Dakota. Sorry, I have been a bit out of sorts. But I'll try and pop in on you at work on Saturday. You don't have to give me anything. It'll just be nice to spend time together."

Dakota smiled when I told her that. "That sounds good," she said. We got told to get on with our work.

Jennifer always sits next to Dominic Green in science. It was the first time I'd seen them together before Chloe told me about him lying to the boys. They were talking quietly, gradually getting louder, out of nowhere, Jennifer stood up and hurried out of the classroom right in the middle of the lesson! She's always been a bit of a teacher's pet; to her, rules are everything- so if I wasn't there to witness it myself, I would never have believed it happened. Jennifer looked like she was about to cry, and so did Dominic, he looked really miserable after she left. I wondered if I should go after her, but Mr Williams, our teacher, handed out little bottles of chemicals, and I kind of got caught up in the task and working with Dakota.

I asked Mum for money after I got home for when I visit the café on Saturday, and straightaway she began to stress. Mum was cooking tea, complained about money being tight and asked whether it was important. Not a great start. I had to lay it on a bit thick to get what I needed.

"Well, it's to be with friends. You want me to hang out and have friends, don't you?"

Mum turned on the hob to cook dried spaghetti. "Can you not just go to each other's houses and play the PlayStation or something?"

"No one plays the PlayStation anymore, Mum."

"Right, sorry." She grabbed her bag, already flustered.

"It's okay, I'll not go, stay home again. I'm kind of getting used to it now anyway." I walked away as I spoke and kept my head down. I pretended to wipe a tear from my eye.

It worked, though.

"No, wait, let me see how much I got."

I stopped and turned around as she rooted around in her purse. She went upstairs and found Mac to ask how much cash he had as she only had a fiver. I ended up with £20, which should be enough for a few shakes, a meal, and maybe even the cinema if Dakota can go. Result!

Thank goodness it's Friday! I had double Maths today, which was intense! We did past exam papers as we have mock exams coming in mid-November. I didn't do well, and my teacher Miss Selby didn't look very pleased. She said I was one of her brightest students last year, and I needed to focus on work. She's right, but I keep finding I can't concentrate and remember things. I try to finish all my homework and follow the lessons, but the task seems enormous and unobtainable.

Chloe, who sits with me, got less than seven wrong on each paper! Miss Selby suggested we help each other and maybe study together. Chloe looked at me with raised eyebrows, "well, do you want to? Judging by these, you probably need all the help you can get!"

I shrugged, "I don't know, maybe."

"Well, you're the one who needs help, Augusta. But if you want to study, I'm willing to give up a few lunchtimes for you. We can do it in the library."

"Okay."

"Cool. WhatsApp me, okay? And we'll arrange one for next week."

I smiled. I felt good and very productive.

After Maths, I had Art which was nice. I always enjoy Art. It's where I'm most natural, and I don't have to think. I draw, paint, and express myself. There are no wrong answers. My teacher, Mr Paulson, likes practically everything I do, so I get lots of praise.

At the end of the day, I had PE. My worst subject. It is so much work and too much exercise. I knew we'd be running around and constantly worrying about sweating. I sweat a lot, and patches appear on my clothes, so everyone knows I'm smelly and unclean. It's really embarrassing. I am with Dakota for PE, and when I saw her today, I noticed her breasts have grown. She had a gorgeous bra on, too, that suited her really well.

I saw Thai across from us. She was undressing too. Her breasts looked small but in proportion, and she had a washboard stomach. She looked like an athlete. Thai didn't even look at me when she said, "everyone knows you're staring. Everyone is watching you, knowing what you are thinking."

I looked around me nervously; people were pretending not to listen. I could feel my face burn up and get hot.

Dakota touched my arm and said, "What's the matter with you?"
I shook my head and murmured, "I don't know." I quickly got dressed.
"Ready?"

I followed her lead by acting like nothing had happened. I didn't want to embarrass her, so I said nothing as we ran downstairs to play hockey. Tamara hit my ankle with her stick. I think it was on purpose! I have a big bruise there now; it's going to leave a massive bump. I hope it doesn't hurt too much, and I'm still okay with seeing Dakota tomorrow.

I have so much homework to do. But the mere thought of it is so overwhelming. I try to get my brain to work, but it's not connecting. I have to write an essay on 'How has crime and punishment changed in Britain between 1250 and 1900?'

Who makes up these questions? It feels so vague! Describe what happened in the space of 650 years. A lot, I'm guessing!

I like gangster films and I had my fingers crossed Al Capone was in there so I could describe the St Valentine's Day Massacre for most of the topic. But when I looked, apparently that was in the 1920s, so a little later. A bit tight of them not to include him.

I googled the entire question, typed the whole thing in the search bar to see if I could get some ideas. Apparently, there was a lot of whipping and branding and being dragged on the ground by a horse. It was before TV, so they had to amuse themselves somehow.

I know Jack the Ripper was before 1900. And Henry VIII was in the mid-1500s, so thanks to the rhyme divorced, beheaded, died, divorced, beheaded, survived, I know beheadings and hanging must be in the middle. Quite a horror show.

So far, I have; Time changes everything. Including crime. Where there is a crime, there are consequences, so people were punished. But were they guilty? No one knows because, in the 1200s, they did not have detectives or forensic analysis like we do today. They burnt women for being witches, and this totally held back feminism by some years. There were no police, so people got away with stuff.

Now I'm stuck. I'll have to google more stuff on Sunday. That's enough for now.

I moved on to French. Tenses. Perfect tense or imperfect? Fifty-fifty. Bit easier. I alternated my choice of the two down the sheet, the whole thing is in French, and I haven't got the energy to look at it all properly. The second part is conjugating verbs. I googled 'conjugate' (Give different forms). This is no help, so I also put this away till Sunday.

Proud of all my hard work, I lie back on my bed. I have a lot more piled up, but I can't be bothered with it. Why do they give us so much? I will have to try again with another subject in a minute. I leant over to look at Maths. Worksheets. A mock paper. I'm in hell. Maybe I can do it on Monday with Chloe, improving my chances a bit. After Maths, I have Science, English, Ethics and Philosophy, and some for drama and Art. Bored of it all now.

Mum and Mac always complain that I don't spend enough time with them and never go to clubs or anywhere beyond our home. But with homework and other pressure, how can they expect me to fit in everything? I am one person. How does Dakota fit in a job as well? I think I'm dumb as I struggle to try and finish it all before the assignments are due back in. School is so intense, and they want us to revise on top of all this! Help!

At last, it's time to see Dakota. She said to pop over at about 10ish before the lunchtime rush. I woke up early to work out my outfit- I decided on a black baggy hoodie and jeans. I do my hair a bit, but it droops down my face, all dreary and dull.

I spent hours at the café. Dakota kept having to serve but chatted when she could. Her boss, Gene, is pretty laid back, but he has this massive crush on her, so we call him Gene the Sleaze. He licks his lips a lot whenever he is talking to her. It's gross.

Dakota told me she was going to the beach later if I wanted to come. I asked who was going, and she said, "Oh, just the usual crowd."

It occurred to me that we never had a crowd before. It was only us—Dakota and me. I thought, when did they become 'the usual crowd'? Am I considered one of them? Did I become part of a crowd without being aware of it?

I guess she means Jamie, Johanna, and all that lot.

"Rosie likes you," Dakota told me. "And I promise I won't go off with J. I'll be with you all night."

"Okay."

So, it looks like I'm going there now. I
don't know what to expect at all. I hope
it's not too bad. I felt a bit of nausea
from my chocolate milkshakes and
chicken burger. They came back up a
bit. I closed my eyes and swallowed it
back down. I still felt like I would be sick, so I went to the
toilet and got rid of it all. Luckily, I had chewing gum in
my pocket so I could disguise the smell.

I'm scared of having a panic attack in front of
everyone on the beach. I don't usually go to public places
for long periods because I never know how to cope when it
happens. I try and remember to breathe, but it feels like
I'm going to die.

It's happening more and more nowadays, and I don't
know how to stop them. The thought of one coming while
everyone is there makes me feel queasy. My right hand
began to shake. Maybe I shouldn't go and stay in bed.
Should I message Dakota? It's not too late.

I feel horrific, so poorly.

My head seems to tear apart with only the slightest movement. I can't even lay down and watch TV. The light from the screen and the sound, no matter how low, is agonising. My curtains are pulled as I can't cope.

I did go last night. I walked over to Dakota's, as Jamie's brother was going to pick us up. Although it was the last day of September, it was summery and warm. I wore a hoodie and jeans, and I made sure it was another black one so they couldn't see any sweat patches. I had plenty of tissues as I was so hot, and I had to keep wiping my face. Although, we were outside, I felt like I was in a sauna, I was hoping it would be cooler on the beach. A bit of natural air conditioning from the sea breeze. Dakota had denim shorts on, and a blue hoodie. As always, she looked great. As the sun hit the streaks in her hair, they became a brilliant shade of red which looked so pretty.

Our lift arrived, and Jamie got out. He kissed Dakota hello, and I wondered if I was ever going to get used to seeing them together. He stepped forward and opened up the back door for us.

"You look great, D," he said as Dakota got in beside me, and she said, "thank you".

Jamie sat next to his brother in the front. I couldn't see much of his brother's appearance as I sat directly behind him. They talked all the way there, and I wondered if I should start a conversation with Dakota, but I didn't know what to say. The palms of my hands were sweating, so I pretended to scratch my leg and rubbed them on my jeans. I looked at Dakota to see if she noticed, but she was quietly staring out at the scenery as we drove by. So, I did too. I undid my window, and the onslaught of wind that greeted me from the car's traction felt so liberating. I closed my eyes and let my hair feel the air. As the wind blew wildly, every strand from my roots on my head were frantically flapping with the force of nature. It was enormously exhilarating and gave me a feeling of being free.

When we finally got there, we found the others relatively quickly after we began to walk along the beach. Dakota and Jamie were strolling hand in hand. I doubted she'd keep her promise and stay with me, but as soon as Jamie saw Tucker and Zayn playing football on the sand; he let go of Dakota's hand, and ran over to join them, leaving Dakota and me alone.

Johanna, Renee, and Tamara had triangular bikini tops and tiny little ripped shorts lying down on towels. But, of course, they all had perfect bodies, and I was glad I didn't even think about wearing my swimming costume today. Each of them was brown and olive-skinned, whereas I am so white. My body looks nothing like theirs; I would stand out a mile for all the wrong reasons!

Dakota suggested we look for a good place to settle, build a fire, and collect some sticks. So, we walked along the sand and chatted while keeping an eye out for driftwood. We found loads and carried it all near where the girls were still sunbathing.

Along the way, down further toward the sea, we found a long log that would make an excellent makeshift bench. We went back to it, and both chose an end. Unfortunately, it was heavier than we thought. Luckily, help was coming.

"Hey guys, let us dry off, and we'll give you a hand!" It was Luca. He was walking up from the water with Rosie, wet from swimming. Again, perfect tanned bodies and I wondered how they got like this? I know I don't work out and eat a lot of junk, but they seem to be born with it. I've seen them eat chocolate, yet their skin is pristine, and they have models' body shapes- I don't get it.

It wasn't long before they both joined us wearing towel ponchos. Even in those, they looked fantastic. Luca stood beside me and said, "move to the centre and lift from the middle." Rosie and Dakota took the weight on the other end. Between the four of us, we managed it, and when we got closer to the others, they praised our find, as we lay it down near the firewood. Luca called Jamie over to help look for big rocks to sit on and surround the fire. Zayn and Tucker offered to help too.

"Wow, look at all that wood!" Zayn said. He looked like a model. His skin and body glowed golden in the sun. It reminded me of Twilight when you see Edward full of diamonds. He seemed almost godly. "You guys get all that?"

"There are lots of bits of wood around. You have to look for it." I answered, surprised at myself for sounding so casual in front of a small group.

He smiled at me, showing me his perfect teeth, and patted my shoulder, saying, "good job." I couldn't help but smile back.

"Girls, you put all the wood in the middle, and we'll go get the rocks," Luca instructed as the boys went off. "You guys help too," he called to Johanna, Tamara, and Renee. Rosie, Dakota, and made a pile with the wood. There was more than enough, so we had a nice stack to enable us to top up during the night when we needed it. The lads found a nice supply of rocks, and it all looked quite impressive by the time we finished.

Tucker took a lighter from his pocket and tried to ignite the fire, but the wood wouldn't light. At Jamie's suggestion, we all looked through our pockets and bags to find receipts so we could help it along. I spotted and uprooted some grass near the car park, which allowed the fire to catch along with the bits of scrunched-up paper. We got more and put it around and in between the wood. Our plan worked, and the fire got going. We all whooped and cheered, happy with our team effort.

Jamie sat on one side of the flames with Luca and Rosie, and Dakota sat opposite them next to me. Zayn and Tucker stood over on one side chatting. It was a while before Johanna, Tamara, and Renee came over to join us. The sun had completely clouded over and began to set. As the evening air came, people put jumpers and hoodies on to keep warm. Dakota and I stayed the same. Zayn sat down with Jamie closer to the flames to keep warm.

After everyone gathered around the fire, Tucker and Tamara were smoking and asked everyone if we wanted to liven things up. They held up a bottle of vodka like a trophy, and people cheered and started laughing.

"Don't feel like you have to do anything you don't want to," Dakota said to me quietly.

"Who's having some!?!" Tucker yelled. He took a swig straight from the bottle; Renee called him something I couldn't catch and began rummaging in a carrier bag. She took out a tower of plastic cups. Tamara lined them up on the sand, and Tucker poured out the vodka.

As Renee handed a couple of cups to us, Rosie came over with a bottle of OJ. "Here," she said, pouring some juice. "A lot of us girls don't like it neat."

She tipped a small amount in each cup. "Can I have a bit more in mine?" asked Dakota.

"Sure," said Rosie pouring in some more orange juice.

"Can I have some more too?" I asked her.

Rosie smiled and gave me more as well. "You know what? I think I'll pour a bit more into mine too. Less of a bite."

Rosie was the first to drink. I watched Dakota, curious to see what she would do or say. Dakota drank it. I've never seen her drink alcohol before. She avoided eye contact with me as she did so. I looked at the citrusy liquid in my cup.

"What's the matter, Augusta? Not a big drinker?" Tamara shouted in front of everyone. I put the cup to my lips, closed my eyes and kept gulping it down before I could overthink it. I was not too fond of the taste, so I pretended it was only orange juice. When I had finished, Tucker and Tamara cheered and giggled. "Go, Augusta!" they teased.

To my surprise, Tucker came over with the bottle again, "Here, let's top you up."

Rosie poured in some orange juice. "Take it easy, okay? Try and go slowly, sip this one," she said softly, and sat on the log beside me.

Throughout the night, as soon as our cups were empty, Tucker and Tamara filled them up. When I sipped the second one it was much better, and I began to relax. Tucker was funny, and I felt safe sitting between Dakota and Rosie. Everyone seemed to be in good spirits, talking freely, and having fun.

At one point, Jamie asked Dakota if she wanted to join him and take a walk along the beach. Luca suggested to Rosie that they tag along. Dakota looked at me and asked if it was okay. I nodded, so Dakota and Rosie agreed and left me exposed sat on the log. Renee took Rosie's place and sat on my right. I can't remember anything Renee said, but there were lots of murmurings about me being her mate and she kept putting her arm around me.

Johanna was busy talking to Zayn, and Tamara was still chatting to Tucker, laughing and giggling. They kept touching each other, and soon Tamara and Tucker were kissing. I looked at Johanna. She whispered something in Zayn's ear, and her hand touched his leg. I thought they would kiss too, but Zayn removed her hand and got up, saying he would find the others. He asked if I wanted to come, but Renee pulled me toward her and said, "NO! She's staying with me."

I didn't know what to say. I wanted to go with Zayn, but he ran off down the beach so fast that I couldn't see him. I didn't want to look for the others in the dark on my own. And I felt a bit sick.

Joanna reached for the vodka bottle and found it was empty. She told Tucker off for using it all, but he was too busy with his tongue down Tamara's throat to listen to her. Johanna started swearing and yelling, but I didn't understand what she was trying to say as all her words melted into one, not making much sense.

I felt a bit awkward and wished Dakota would come back. I was uncomfortable, Johanna screamed abuse and pointed straight at me, but I had no idea what she was saying, so I couldn't respond in any way. Finally, Renee told her to calm down, and they shouted at each other arguing. Then I saw Thai, and I focused on her. Although it was dark, she was radiant and bright, and I could see her so clearly. She waved hello, and said, "you should do something."

"I don't know what to do," I told her.

She didn't break eye contact or even blink. Those dazzling sea-green eyes hypnotised me. "Think of something. You're coming off as a bit weird and also a complete idiot."

I lost my temper.

"IT'S NOT MY FAULT! I DON'T KNOW WHAT I AM SUPPOSED TO DO, DO I!?!"

Suddenly Renee's face came into my view as she tried to get my attention. "Augusta?" Her hands waved over my face, "Augusta?"

I looked at her.

"Hey!" she said. "Who are you talking to?"

I blinked. Everyone was silent and staring at me, including Tamara and Tucker, who had stopped kissing.

I pointed to Thai. "Her," bellowed.

Thai pointed to herself as if to say *Who me?* And she began to laugh.

"Oh my God, you are so weird," Johanna said as she staggered up. "I need to get out of here before you all drive me crazy! I'm going for a swim. It's too hot." She walked away like a little kid who'd been spinning on the spot for 10 minutes, and straight away disappeared from view.

Renee got up and ran after her, and I heard her shout, "Johanna! Wait! You're drunk!" as she followed her into the darkness.

"I'm worried. I think we should follow her." Tamara said, gazing up at Tucker.

Tucker rolled his eyes, "Great." He said sarcastically. "Come on then, let's stop the silly bint before she drowns herself." They held hands and walked off. Tamara looked at me weird as she went past.

I was alone with the fire. Thai had disappeared at some point, probably gone to find Johanna too. I don't know how long it was before the others came back.

"Where is everyone?" asked Luca.

"Johanna got drunk and wandered off. So, they all went to try and find her," I answered.

Rosie told him they better look too.

"You okay to go?" Dakota asked me.

"Yeah," but as I got up, I wobbled and fell on the sand. I cracked up laughing. Zayn came over to me and scooped me up in his arms. "Come here, " he said, holding me close to his chest. "Let's get you to the car."
Jamie's brother was already waiting. They must have messaged him on their walk. I felt Zayn drop me into the seat gently, put my seat belt on, and kiss my forehead, wishing me goodnight.

I don't remember trying to sleep when I finally got into my bed last night. I think I dropped off as soon as my head hit the pillow. However, when I woke up this morning, it felt like my head was pulsating and trying to escape from my brain. I am in a world of utter misery.

I told Mum and Mac I got my period; they took pity on me and made fried egg sandwiches. I've kept topping up my glasses of water and have stayed in my bed all day. I am never touching vodka again!

Sorry, it's been a while since I last wrote. There's been nothing to report until now. I know the idea is to write every day, but I've been tired from homework and stuff.

Jennifer was suffering in Drama on Monday. She was so quiet; she didn't suggest any ideas for our work or anything. It's like she's become a different person. Mrs Kenyon noticed and asked her if she was okay. Jennifer didn't even answer. Chloe put her arm around her and told Mrs Kenyon it was the first day of her period. I smoothed her arm, but she didn't react. Jennifer seemed like a body without a soul, almost like joy had been sucked out of her. Mrs Kenyon told her to sit quietly and do the best she could.

I heard the following day that it had kicked off that afternoon. When we first came in in Form group and registration, Chloe told me that Jennifer's twin Jude punched Dominic Green in the playground. Mr Farthing, the PE teacher, saw them and moved Jude away before he could get in another swing. Jude has been suspended. Dominic wasn't in Form or French, so I don't know if he was as well.

We were all given a letter to take home. There is a school trip abroad to Italy skiing for five days in February. I've always wanted to go to Italy. It looks beautiful, arty, and cultured. I heard you don't sweat as the heat from the sun is different from the weather here. How amazing is that? Sunny days and no worries about sweat patches!?! Amazing! Plus, I love pizza, and I've never been abroad before. Lots of my friends have been to Spain, France, and Portugal, but I have never been.

But, surprise, surprise, I can't go. The cost was £1328, and Mum said she couldn't afford it. I argued you can pay in instalments, but it was still a firm "No." Mac offered to pay half, but Mum said she felt terrible letting him do that when Dad can't afford to pay anything.

Mum couldn't afford a new place on her own when they broke up, which is why Dad is in his tiny flat. I've lived here since I was born. As only a few years were left on the mortgage, they felt it was silly to sell the house, and both ended up renting. They both want to leave the house to me and are convinced house prices will go up, so Mum and Dad are making sacrifices now so I can get on the property ladder.

Mum and Dad pay half the mortgage each month, and at home, Mum and Mac split the bills. Unfortunately, my dad can only afford a small place after his portion of the mortgage and his other bills are paid, which I feel bad about. I know they are doing all this for me, but I miss out on so much. Like this ski trip which everyone else in my entire year is going on.

I've wanted a pair of Air Jordans for TWO YEARS, and I am still waiting. Seeing other kids strut around in new trainers, Air Jordans, and Beats headphones is harsh; I've got the same old Nike Air Max from a year ago. I have cheap crappy buds that came free with my mp3 player. Everyone I know has an iPhone, whereas I have a boring bog-standard contract one. Their music players are iPods, and mine is a ZenZi one that Mum got from a catalogue so she could spread payments.

Yet when I'm given rubbish budget presents, they expect me to be happy and grateful and go nuts over it! I know Mum and Dad are trying their best, but Zenzi is not Apple, and Nike Air Max is not the same as Air Jordans. They might not be able to tell the difference, but I can, and so can every other kid in my school.

Chloe was talking to me about it when we got handed the letters. She thinks her parents will be awkward about the price too, so Chloe plans to work and try to pay half or at least contribute to it so she can go. Her Uncle is a landlord at a pub and promised if Chloe ever wanted a job, there would be one in the kitchen washing dishes and doing small cookery bits. Chloe had never accepted the offer before because he was looking for someone on Thursdays, Fridays, Saturdays, and Sunday dinnertimes, and she thought it would be too much with schoolwork and dance classes. But Italy is way too good an opportunity to pass up! Chloe's never been abroad before either.

Maybe I should do the same and try to get a job with Dakota. The only thing is, I don't want a Gene the Sleaze leering all over me. Dakota's working so she can get a car. She said I could use it too once I learned how to drive. We're not even 16 yet, but Dakota said lessons and a car are expensive. Her parents have money, so I said they'd be willing to pay, but Dakota said she wanted to earn the car herself. I don't get that at all. If someone is willing to pay, why not accept the help? Parents are there to support us in any way they can.

She's letting them pay for the skiing trip, though, I asked at breaktime. She said, "That's different. That's school stuff."

I don't know how Dakota has time to work. She's been doing it for over a year now. All her money goes into a savings account her dad set up for her. It feels like she's juggling way too much.

Dakota doesn't know what she wants to be. I don't either. Some kids do and have it together, but there are so few jobs now. What if I study and study, get qualified in my chosen field, and what I want to do isn't available? Or I can't get work of any kind. How would I earn a living? There are no fail-safe options, so what if I make all the wrong choices about getting educated in the subjects that give me the best chance? Would it be better to go out, try to find a job, and work my way up, forgetting university altogether? I have to make these decisions soon, and I am terrified.

We've all been too busy being a kid; this pivotal moment in our lives has crept in without us noticing, and now we have to act.

I read this book last year in English, The Catcher in the Rye, and for most of it, I was pretty bored, but there was one part that stuck in my head. The main character, this kid, was in a cornfield at the edge of a cliff. All these children were running toward him, and he had to save them all. Like, all at once. Everyone and everything came at him. The pressure of so much all at the same time made it hard for him to cope. He wants to do the right thing and save them, but it's hard. Life and its expectations are too much. That's how I feel.

Right now, I am losing so many- I am not saving any of them. I am failing, and I need help. Everything is falling, I am failing, and I can do nothing to stop it.

It was Mum's birthday yesterday; my Gran was here. She always asks me the same things:

-Do you like school? (Seriously, who does?)

-Have you got a boyfriend? (☹ Nope, no one loves me! Thanks for the reminder, Gran!)

-What would I like for Christmas this year? (Months away, she only pops a fiver in an envelope anyway.)

And lastly,

-How am I coping after my little 'episode'?

I never know what to say, so I answer, "I guess," and hope she moves on.

I did Mum a portrait of me, her, and Mac for her present. She loved it and cried as soon as she saw it. It didn't take me overly long, but mums seem to love anything homemade.

Mac bought and passed me a card to give to Mum the night before. Unfortunately, Dad did the same thing, so I had to give her dads later in the day. I explained why she was getting two cards when we were alone in the kitchen, and she said I was being very considerate to Mac's feelings, which was lovely of me.

We had a Chinese delivered and ate some birthday cake Mac had made for her. It was red velvet, her absolute favourite, and what he has baked for her on every birthday they have spent together. Mum reminds us every time! I ate loads, felt full and decided to have a bath as it was warm in the house, and I felt my body becoming a bit sweaty. So, I filled the tub high and sunk my face under the water.

I got out, dried myself off with the towel, and went into Mum and Mac's room to borrow some deodorant as I had run out. They have full-length mirrors on their wardrobe doors, and when I passed by, I saw myself. I looked disgusting. My bones were sticking out all over the place, and spots were dotted all over my body.

And there was hair, so much hair everywhere. Under my arms, on my arms, on and between my legs, even on my toes! I felt sick to my stomach. I was repulsed and appalled at how hideous and freaky I looked. I had to act.

The only thing I could do right now was get rid of all this grotesque disgusting mass of cruddy black infestation. I returned to the bathroom, found Mac's razor, back into their bedroom and started shaving. I couldn't get rid of the hair fast enough. I panicked, scraping, shearing wildly to remove this contamination from my body, working ferociously on my arms and legs.

They began to burn and bleed. I wiped away the blood with the razor; I wanted all the hair to disappear. I was crying hysterically as I worked.

I hated myself. Why do I look like this? Why can't I look normal?

How can I stop my ugly spiteful body from flaunting its barbaric merciless nature? How can I stop it from being hostile, tearing me down savagely day after day?

I saw a mole with hair growing from it; I tried digging it out, but I couldn't see what I was doing. Blood kept flooding over my arm. My body was on fire and so sore.

I could feel the crimson liquid leaking, flowing free, stinging my legs as it ran down onto the carpet. I heard a scream. I wasn't even sure if it came from me. It didn't.

"MAC!"

Mum.

"MAC!"

She was crying, struggling to hold my hands firmly together. In the end, Mum turned my body around and pulled my arms behind me.

I heard footsteps thundering up the stairs as Mac came in.

"There's blood everywhere!" Mum said between sobbing. "Get the razor from her hand. QUICK! MAC!"

Mum must have seen me trying to get rid of it all. My hand didn't want to let go of my weapon, my armour against this contagion invading my body. This razor was my only route to try and abolish a piece of repulsive monstrosity. How could they ask me to give up my one defence? I was determined not to let go.

However, Mac is strong and prised my fingers apart, I felt despair as the razor helplessly dropped to the floor. Mac scooped me up, carried me into the bathroom, and placed me back in the bath. Raw fire plagued my body.

Mum held my hands firmly under the water. "You're okay, sweetheart. You're okay."

I felt numb. Thoughtless. Scared. In agony.

"I'll give you guys some time," Mac said quietly. I heard his footsteps stop outside the door.

Mum's voice broke as she spoke to me. "Why would you do that to yourself? You know we love you so much."

"I'm disgusting."

Fresh tears rolled down my mum's face.

"You are beautiful," she told me. "I know you may not feel it right now, but you are. I've never lied to you, even when you asked the most difficult questions." She stroked the back of my head. "So, believe me when I say you are the most beautiful girl I have seen."

I can't be something I'm not. "I'm ugly." I moved my hands away from hers and curled into a ball.

"Augusta, it breaks my heart that you are in so much pain." Mum lifted my hands gently and held them together, with hers. "You think you know so much about the world, how people see you. But there is one thing you do not realise. I am in complete awe of you."

I looked at her, wondering if I had finally driven her mad.

Mum looked deep into my eyes as she spoke. "Every day, you get up, and you keep going. The worst thing as a mum is watching your child go through suffering, watching them torment themselves. Knowing you are helpless to stop it. The scary thing is, I don't even know the depths of what you are going through, and I doubt you do either. It kills me I can't fully understand. I want to help you so badly, but as I don't know how to, all I can do is promise you two things."

Mum cupped her hands and poured water over me, so I didn't get cold as she continued talking.

"One. I will be by your side and fight for you to become who I know you are underneath all this turmoil and unrest.

You see, I already know that part. I know who you can be, and Darling- it's spectacular. I can't wait for you to get there and finally understand how genuinely awe-inspiring you really are.

And two. As much as it seems there is no end to feeling rubbish right now, and everything is piling on top of you, this time will not last. Things WILL change. You will change, and your life WILL get easier.

Anything worth having comes from a rocky road, but you have love and support. Me, Mac, your dad, Dakota, and Gran, we all love you and be holding your hand the whole way.

As I never lie to you, that means those two things are true. And also, that you are, in fact, beautiful." Mum smiled. "Plus, it's my birthday, so you have to believe everything I say."

Mum hugged me, even though I was lying in a bathtub full of lukewarm water, which was now red. She got a fresh towel from the airing cupboard, and told Mac, "She's okay, " before returning with body lotion. Mum dried me, gently rubbed the cream all over to ease the cuts and told me to stay put for a second as she was going to get a comb and some pyjamas.

While Mum was gone, I saw the label on the lotion used to soothe my skin. It was this expensive honey stuff Gran had given her for her birthday. I didn't say anything or let on I knew.

Mum returned with fresh underwear, the comb, and the pair of long cotton eggshell blue pyjamas she gave me last Christmas Eve. Mum dressed me, and I let her, even though I could dress myself. The cotton felt fresh against my skin. When we came out, I heard scrubbing from their bedroom and sponges splashing with water. I guessed Mac was trying to get the blood stains out from the carpet. I sat on my bed, and my mum combed through my hair.

"I'm sorry I ruined your birthday Mum," I told her. "I am thankful for every minute we have together, Augusta, good or bad. If we are together, I don't need anything else."

Every so often, you have a defining connection with another person where you are truly grateful for that moment. It seems to be when you share words or a flash of friendship, and there is a sort of epiphany that all you need or want in life is to have these little snapshots of time. The people you are with suddenly shares an unspoken bond with you, as the whole world will only experience that precise minute a single time. And together you made that one count.

We usually waste so many that we forget we have one chance to live at that exact point in humankind's history.

When we make the most of those unique minutes, we feel good. Sometimes, we forget about it in a month, a year or even a week. But other times, you treasure them and remember the little connections and feel a slight glow inside of you as you experience them again.

It felt like one of these times for Mum and me. I looked at her and felt so much love. I am so glad she's mine. If I had to choose anyone to be my mum, it would be her. I wouldn't even have to think.

When I had my 'blip', she asked me why.

It pains me now to think about it. You see, I always felt so alone. In my thoughts, who I was, so alienated and isolated from the rest of the world. People can underestimate the power of loneliness; it can consume you. Dominate your existence, perspective and belief in yourself and others. You never get over the feeling no one wants to be around you.

When you have rabbits, they need to be in groups and pairs. When they lose their friend, rabbits can get sick from loneliness and die from a broken heart. They have to form a bond with each other to survive.

Humans aren't that different. We need contact, which is why social media is so addictive, and we can't bear to be away from our phones. We yearn for a connection with another human being.

At times like this, I feel guilty because Mum is trying so hard to make sure I know I am not alone, and she is there for me. But sometimes, a mother's love isn't enough. I need more.

So, when she asked me why I did it, instead of telling her this, that like me, no matter how hard she tried, Mum would constantly be failing, I told her a different truth.

"I was tired of holding on, struggling to get through each day. Finally, I wasn't brave enough to fight anymore, and I couldn't find another way to surrender."

I couldn't talk about yesterday on the day. It was too much. So, I stayed in bed with the covers up.

Something happened in French class. There is a new girl in school, Jenna Dawson. She is massive and is the size of a female wrestler- big, wide, and tall. My teacher, Miss Rhodes, introduced her in front of the class and told her to take a seat.

Unfortunately for me, Miss Rhodes spotted me scrolling through Instagram on my phone and said, "Augusta, phone, please." When I paused, she said, "Now, Augusta." I had to give it to her- I only got it back from the office this morning.

But when she said my name, Jenna Dawson screeched, "Aw! What a name! Auggy Fugly", and she began laughing hysterically.

The whole class hooted noisily, and kept repeating, "Auggy Fugly! Auggy Fugly". They stood up, rejoicing, and pointing. I looked at Dakota, her head was down fixated on our desk, pretending not to hear. My best friend in the world was ignoring what was happening—ignoring me.

A ball of paper hit my head, followed by something hard. "Auggy Fugly!" I looked at the floor to see what hit me, and it was a Snickers bar. Someone had thrown an actual Snickers at me.

They chanted repeatedly on a continuous endless loop,

"Auggy Fugly! Fucking ugly! Auggy Fugly! Fucking Ugly!" Over and over.

A lump was firmly in my throat. My body felt fuzzy, and my face felt numb. I looked at Miss Rhodes, begging her in my head, screaming at her, *DO SOMETHING!!!!!* Oblivious to my pleas, she continued to look away. The vicious taunting got louder. I stared at Miss Rhodes more intensely, desperate for the message to get through. *HELP ME! YOU'RE MY TEACHER. YOU ARE MEANT TO PROTECT ME!*

I hopelessly tried to add volume, and out of frustration, I slapped my hand hard on my desk. Miss Rhodes finally looked at me. Barely more than a whisper, I managed, "Miss. Help. Please." But she couldn't hear. Or chose not to. My cries were met with silence. Instead, my teacher let it happen.

The taunting got louder.

"AUGGY FUGLY! FUCKING UGLY! AUGGY FUGLY! FUCKING UGLY!"

I couldn't take it anymore. Out of despair, I grabbed my bag and ran out of the classroom to savage cheering and brutal laughter. I could hear animalistic howling down the corridor.

I have known people in that class since year 7. We worked on projects together and hung out as friends. How could they turn on me like that without a second thought? I hate Jenna Dawson. I hate her.

I needed to get as far away as possible; tears continually streamed down my face. I ran down the street, trying to get as far away from school as possible.

Eventually, I slowed down, walked to the town park, and sat on a bench. I realised I had left my French book on my desk.

On the play equipment, there was a toddler, a little boy with his Mum. I envied him. I wanted to be spontaneous, uninhibited, carefree, untroubled, and happy like him. Happy most of all. I can't remember the last time I genuinely was.

On the grass, I saw Thai playing a guitar. She looked perfect as usual. Strangely, I wasn't surprised to see her there or to see Thai playing her guitar.

"You are alone again," she sang.

"And ugly. So ugly, no one wants to be with you. You could spend forever alone, and nobody would care. You have no friends, no place in this world. Alone again, so ugly, and alone."

She packed away her guitar and quietly walked away. I came home at the usual time. If Mum or Mac knew I wasn't in school, they didn't let on. I went upstairs and got into bed.

Today, I kept my head down and rushed to my classes. I spent lunch and break time in the toilet, staring at the cubicle door.

I didn't eat till I came home. Some people said, "Alright, Fugly?" as I passed, but I ignored them.

About 80 minutes ago, Chloe sent me a message and a link on WhatsApp. 'I'm so sorry to show you this, Augusta, but I thought you should know.' I clicked on the link; it was a TikTok video by Violet Richards. I knew Violet, but not well. She was a girl in my year. Dance music with flashes played, and in the centre was a grainy picture of me in school uniform- I guess she used the year 10 photo the school took for our parents last year. The camera zoomed in and out on my face, and a chant of "Auggy Fugly!" repeatedly shouting. The voice was Jenna Dawson, so they must have made it together. It already had 712 views and 43 likes. I went into the bathroom and threw up in the toilet.

It's been a week. So many people are still watching the video, I hear the music everywhere at school along with people laughing. I still can't face anyone, so I have continued my strategy of rushing to classes and spending quality time inside the Ladies. Today I heard Thai outside the door. "Everyone's talking about you. They can't stop laughing about Auggy Fugly."

I cried and put my lunch in the bin meant for sanitary towels. Afterwards, I forced myself to go to all my classes apart from French. I don't have my French book, and I can't go back. Especially knowing Jenna Dawson will be there. Chloe asked me about studying together in the library for maths, but I said I wasn't sure. The thought of people wandering about whispering and staring at me isn't overly appealing.

"Don't hide away, Augusta," she said while we were trying to study quadratic equations. "It'll all blow over. You'll see."

I don't think it will.

In Art, I had to show Mr Paulson my portfolio so far. He thought it was good work, but he said it was way too dark. I told him I always did dark stuff; that's my style and what I like.

"I understand that, but Augusta, this is on another level. You always produce work from the heart as a form of expression. Your honesty and willingness to put so much vulnerability into your work make you an exceptional student. But this is so deep." He said, "if ever you need to talk, my door is always open. Or you can come here and paint anytime, let me know and I can arrange something. I am always here to help you any way I can."

He is nice, Mr Paulson, but what can he do in reality? Teachers don't want to get involved. Look at Miss Rhodes if you need an example. How can he possibly understand any of it? See, that's the thing- nobody can do anything to help me. Dakota keeps her head down. Mum can hardly stay with me all day- both she and Mac have jobs. I am alone. I don't sleep or eat. I am miserable and a joke to everyone and everything. Worst of all, I don't know how to be anything else and make anything different. I need it all to stop.

 I checked out Johanna Robinson's Instagram tonight. She's got 3,817 followers. The feed is full of pics of her in a bikini or posed in chunky jumpers pouting to the camera. There are loads of pictures of her with Tamara and Renee pretending to kiss and different group shots.

I scrolled through and saw her. I stopped. There's a photo of Johanna with Renee, Tamara, Rosie, Luca, Zayn, Tucker, Jamie, and beside him, my so-called best friend, Dakota. *"The usual crowd."*

Everyone is tagged; they are eating fries and burgers. The caption read: 'Making memories with my mates. Love you guys!'

Dakota and I have never said 'love you' to each other. I tapped on comments; there were lots from people I didn't know. Renee put 'the gangs all here x love you guys XXXX. '

My stomach tightened; I saw Dakota comment with a love heart. I guess she loves them all too.

I saw another photo of Tamara, Johanna, Rosie, and Dakota. The caption was 'Besties'. I swiped on a gallery of clothes shopping, getting Starbucks, laughing together, and having fun.

Dakota never messaged me about going for burgers, hanging out in town, shopping, or going anywhere.

I clicked on Rosie's tag to bring up her profile. Predictably, there were lots of photos of her and Luca. Including a cute one doing a Lady and the Tramp thing with an extra-long French fry. 'Thursday night Date night '

I typed Dakota into the search box, we are already friends on Insta, but I hardly ever look up her profile. There were lots of pics of her and Jamie together. Selfies, a D and J with a heart around it etched in the sand, lots of photos of them with her dog BB, and group shots of them with Luca and Rosie bowling and surfing.

I guess she's moved on, outgrown me and our friendship. Dakota and I have been friends since primary school. Stupidly I always thought we would be lifelong friends. Now I find it hard to imagine us hanging out together ever again.

Meredith stuck up for Jennifer in Ethics when Mark and Jeffrey went after her about Dominic. Why did Dakota not do the same? I was left. My best friend abandoned me in my time of need. Are we not as close as Meredith and Jennifer? I believed we were, well, until now obviously.

I couldn't help it; I know I shouldn't, but I opened TikTok. The video has 2082 views now and 102 likes. "Auggy Fugly." That's who I am. What I am. No wonder no one wants to be my friend. If I were them, I wouldn't either.

Mum, Dad, and Mac had to attend a meeting with me in the headmaster's office today. Mrs Wolf went into lecture mode as soon as she established the family dynamic.

"I'm afraid the school is a little concerned about you, Augusta," she began. She was staring right at me. Mrs Wolf has these very thick glasses that make her eyes look massive.

And her mouth has one of those natural frowns. Even when Mrs Wolf is happy with you, she looks annoyed and disappointed. None of the kids likes her particularly. "Your work has dropped in standard from every subject, except Art. However, even Mr Paulson is worried about you, as your work has taken such a dramatic turn. In such an important year, we need to get back on track quickly for you to meet the grades we know you are more than capable of."

Mrs Wolf stared at me. She was waiting, expecting me to react or something. But instead, she asked me if anything was going on at home.

Mum told her I had a 'difficult' summer (Mum promised me she wouldn't say anything about the 'blip'). "Augusta may have been struggling, but there's still time to work things out. We have every faith in her." She smiled at me and squeezed my hand. I smiled and squeezed back.

Mrs Wolf decided to poke her pointy nose in. "May I ask what happened during the summer to make it such a difficult time?"

Mum gave me a look. I shook my head.

Dad spoke, "Augusta isn't quite herself at the moment. She just needs more time." I think Mum told him to steer clear and keep things 'blip' free.

"I'm afraid that's one thing we haven't got, Mr Walsh. Do you both know Augusta has been missing classes?"

Mrs Wolf has landed me in it. I stared at her intensely. I hoped to get my own back by making her feel extremely uncomfortable.

"No, I can assure you we didn't." Mum's voice had an edge to it. I'm in trouble, I could feel Mum's eyes on me, so I immediately looked at the floor.

"So, you can understand our need to bring you in.," Mrs Wolf went on, with a triumphant tone. "To be frank, the whole thing has us a little perplexed. Through your time here, Augusta, you have always been a model student. Your coursework was detailed, well researched, and homework was always on time; all your teachers had nothing but praise for you.

But now we are seeing a completely different girl. Instead of 8's and 9's, you have dropped to an average of 5. I know we are not very far through the year, but as this is a time-sensitive matter, we need to sort it out before things get worse."

"What can we do?" Mac asked.

Mrs Wolf stared at Mac as if she had forgotten he was there. "Well, I'm going to put Augusta on report. Her teachers would have to sign her paper every lesson."

Oh no. French. I can't do French.

"And I'm afraid, Augusta, the rest is up to you." Mrs Wolf stared at me as she spoke. I had to meet her eyes and try not to make it obvious I was staring at the end of her nose as a focal point. Her cold, hard stare was much better than mine. I reckon Mrs Wolf was trying to hypnotise me into telling her all my secrets. Nosey intrusive dragon.

For the parents' benefit, though, the power-hungry Head had to pretend she cared, so she blabbered on. "The time has come for you to sort things out. I know it's, as your parents say, *a difficult time*, but you have to take charge, or you will throw away your future and everything you have worked toward for the last four years. I know you have some real gifts, your Art, your remarkable memory, and ability to recall things in detail, but it will not be enough to guarantee those 8's and 9's you need to get through to your next provision."

Mrs Wolf looked sternly toward each of us in her office. She had the room, and everyone's attention. She was loving it. "I will check that you are doing your homework and handing it in on time, and I will alert your parents and stepfather..."

"Um, we're not married, " Mac interrupted, breaking her little speech.

"Oh, sorry." She sounded a little flustered. I had to stop myself smiling.

Mac waved his hand to let her know it was okay, and Mrs Wolf continued. " As I said, I'll alert people at home if the work is not handed in on time.

So, Mr and Mrs Walsh, and your good self," she nodded to Mac (not sure she knew his name). He smiled politely, signalling Mrs Wolf to go on. "If you could try and keep Augusta focused, make sure she is studying, revising, don't let her get distracted, we may be able to pull this back."

Mum thanked her and told Mrs Wolf she agreed. They all stood up, so I got up too.

Mrs Wolf handed me a yellow leaflet. "Augusta, if ever you need to talk."

The leaflet was for counselling. I shoved it crumpled into my school bag. "Thanks," I said quietly.

"Let's go." Mum said, as she put her arm around me and led me out of Mrs Wolf's office.

They all had to go back to work, so we said goodbye there and Mum, Dad, and Mac, all assured me we could turn things around and not to worry. Luckily for me, my family are still treading carefully after my 'blip'. I think any other kid after that meeting would be grounded for months!

Unfortunately, as well as my family had to get back to work, I had to get to class. So, I decided to forget about it all for now, and hoped to figure out everything later.

Jamie followed me out after Ethics and asked if we could talk. I said, "okay."

So, we walked a little bit and found ourselves on a small path outside the hall.

"Look, D's in bits. She wants to be your friend again, but thinks you hate her. She's sorry about what happened; D doesn't know what to do, or even if you want to see her again. She really feels terrible, Augusta. You guys are so tight. Come on; you're her best friend."

I nodded. I wasn't sure what Jamie wanted me to say. I can't tell him what I think or feel, I don't even know yet.

He stepped forward with his arms open. I crossed my arms tight against my chest, worried he'd try to hug me. But in hindsight, I can see he only wanted to talk. I'm not too sure how to talk to Jamie Parsons. We've barely even spoken.

"Jenna Dawson is a bitch. Zayn and Luca asked her to take down the video, but she's being a bit of a cow and said she'll do what she likes."

I could feel myself starting to cry. If Zayn Lancaster and Luca Young couldn't get her to stop, there was no hope for me. This video will be around forever.

"We're going to try Violet Richards tomorrow," Jamie said. "Hopefully, she'll be a bit more reasonable. I'm so sorry, Augusta. I can't imagine how you must feel. With French and this, life must feel pretty crap at the minute."

I nodded again, more jittery this time; I was trying to hold everything together. I didn't want to cry in front of him and look like this weakling loser who can't stop snivelling.

Jamie touched my arm. I flinched at the sudden burst of human contact and immediately hated myself for reacting that way. No wonder no one wants to become close with me. I'm a freak.

Jamie stepped back to give me space. "Look, you and D have been friends for a long time, and I hope you think of me as a friend now too. Don't ruin all those years of friendship, especially when it's at a time when you need one the most. Think about it." With that, Jamie walked away.

It was nice of him to talk to me; I don't know if Dakota knew or put him up to it. But I think he does care about her a lot.

I saw Dakota in History and tried to get her attention, but she didn't notice or look back. I was willing her to glance my way, but she was concentrated on doing her work. She looked beautiful, but then Dakota always does.

I messaged her when I got home. *'Hey Dakota, Halloween is coming up. Fancy getting together at my place for our yearly ritual of movies and getting loaded on sugar?'* I tried to sound casual but worried I sounded like a dweeb. I sent her the message anyway on WhatsApp and was so nervous she would reject me because it was too late. I also sent a gif of Jack Skellington from *The Nightmare Before Christmas*, as that's our favourite film and an essential part of our classic Halloween night.

I opened the app, and our chat filled my screen, but only one tick meant my message was **Sent** from my phone but not yet **Delivered** to hers. I closed and opened the app again. **One tick.** I turned my phone on and off. **One tick.** It still hadn't been received. I kept refreshing, trying to trick the app, and rebooting it to work. Finally, after what felt like hours, **two ticks. Sent.** I could relax a little.

I checked for ages, but the ticks still hadn't turned blue which means she still hadn't seen it. What was Dakota doing?

I highlighted the message and went up to info. It said '**Read**'. So, she had read it. Dakota didn't want to talk to me. I made a mistake. It was too late, and she didn't know about anything Jamie had said. I felt so stupid. Dakota has new friends now. She's part of the elite. Why would she want to come and hang out with me when she could go shopping, eat burgers, and go to Starbucks? My message was sent 9 minutes ago. I held my finger on it to unsend and save myself any more embarrassment when eventually the blue ticks came, and even better **dots!**

Dakota was **Typing**! Relief!

'I would love to. Thanks for asking me x.'

She's coming! I'm so happy! I rushed downstairs and asked Mum to get toffee apples when she next goes shopping, salty popcorn, and two tubs of Ben and Jerry's Cookie dough ice cream. I was so excited!

I was getting my friend back, and we could spend time just the two of us. Halloween was going to be such a great night! So, straightaway I marked it on the calendar in the kitchen—Saturday *31st October*, Dakota. I can't wait!!!

Mum and Dad ask for my homework planner after every school day.

On Mum's request, Mac brought his whiteboard into the kitchen from his office along with a pad of Post-it notes. Mum marks the days of the week and makes headings for all my different subjects. So, whatever homework I come home with, goes down on Post-it notes and stuck on the day it's due. They also bought me loads of GCSE study books and revision cards, to help me keep track and prepare.

Every day, I have to sit at the kitchen table after tea and go through everything with them for hours. Dad keeps coming over after work. Mac makes himself scarce by going to the gym and leaves it to my parents. It's weird seeing Mum and Dad hanging out so much. I don't think they've spent this much time together since they split.

It's only now, that I see how miserable Mum was. The difference between her with Dad and with Mac is colossal.

She said she had to end it between them because she didn't love Dad anymore. She explained, sometimes, it happens, and it's no one's fault. Dad finds it all quite hard to accept and has never really found his way. About eight months after they separated, Mum met Mac, and they started going out together.

Mum and Dad never even divorced; Mum said she didn't want to put any of us through it and cause any more pain. I thought it was my fault for the longest time. Mum and Dad were always angry with me and upset when it kicked off. Always yelling at me and snapping all the time. It wasn't good. I kept trying to be better, cook and tidy up, as I know that stuff pleases them, so I made my lunches every day for school and packed my own bag. I even cleaned and put on washing. Anything I could think of that might help make them happy to be with me again.

I don't mind if they aren't together anymore. I'm not a sappy, sentimental kid who wants their parents to rekindle. I like Mac, and I like my Mum is happy. I wish my dad would find someone, but it's strange to think of our lives as different from how they are now.

Mac told Mum that he would like them to get a place together and maybe start a family. I don't know if he meant for me to overhear. I know I'm in the way. If I weren't around, it would be easier for them to take their relationship to the next level. But honestly, there's nowhere for me to go. Dad's place is one bedroom, if I went there, he would insist I take the bed, and he would be on the sofa forever. Gran lives at a nursing home, so I can't go there. And there's no one else.

If I could disappear and let them crack on, I would. I'm the one that's to blame for not giving Mum the family she deserves. One day I will make it right.

I have been planning all week. I found my DVDs of The Nightmare Before Christmas and The Greatest Showman. I figured out what to wear- it was a toss-up between chunky slipper socks and boot slippers. I went for slipper socks.

I found a relaxed ponytail style from a TikTok tutorial, and I have been practising it in my room. Mum got all the food I asked her to, and even a bit more, so we now have Pringles and Maltesers. We are all set. Today is Friday. Halloween is just one more sleep.

Today's the day!
Whoop! Whoop!

I got a text from Dakota; she's ill and can't come.

I have read the message about 20 times. My stomach is in knots, and I feel numb. I'm so angry. Why does she have to get sick!?! Why now? Dakota never gets poorly; she has the immune system of a superhero. I have waited for this for SO LONG. I have been patient and understanding about her and Jamie. I have tried so hard!

For goodness ' sake, I hung out with Johanna Robinson and took all her crap! I even reached out after she left me in French class. Why is this happening to me!?! Mum found me crying, and we cuddled on the sofa. She kept asking me to do stuff with her, but I didn't want to talk, eat, go to a cafe or the beach. I only want to stay here, curled up in a ball. Dakota could have come over anyway; I don't mind getting sick. Why is she being so selfish?

I feel so alone. Everything I imagined and prepared was a complete waste of time. It was all for nothing.

Something's happened. Something bad. All on Halloween night.

Mum knew I was disappointed Dakota could not come over, so she tried doing the night anyway, me and her. I know she was trying to be nice, but it wasn't the same, it actually made me feel worse. I know she was doing it out of pity.

I lasted for about an hour, and then I asked Mac to take my place. Instead, I got a change of scenery and went for a walk to clear my head.

I went into town, kids in costumes passed me by, and I could see all the houses decorated in cobwebs, cheap vinyl ghouls, and home-carved pumpkins. I have never tried carving a pumpkin; it looks tough. Some of the pictures you see of the ones people have done on Insta look almost fake; they are that good. I think if I tried, mine would look like a deflated balloon!

There were pots of sweets outside doors, so people weren't disturbed. On the third one I walked by, I looked to see if anyone was about and blindly plunged my hand into the bounty. I brought out a fun-size bag of Skittles which was a bonus. I tore it open and tipped the whole lot into my mouth. It's surprising how many fruit juices flood your senses doing that. It's like the flavours fight for your attention. In the end, they turn into this sickly mass of goo.

I took the clump out and spat it into my hand. It was all white, and a bit gross. I realised I didn't want it anymore, so I poked it through the grill down a nearby drain. My hands were all sticky, so I worked up some saliva and dribbled a bit in my palm and rubbed my hands together. I wiped them on my jeans as I carried on walking.

I wasn't moving with purpose; I was putting one foot in front of the other, not knowing where I was going.

I turned into a street of pretty big houses. I could hear music blaring down the road. I thought I'd check it out. About halfway, I saw a lot of kids hanging around this house. I recognised a couple of boys from my school.

As I got closer, I had to smile; in the middle of the road between the cars was a Jack Skellington and Sally from The Nightmare Before Christmas, it's mine and Dakota's favourite film.

But as I got nearer to them, I began to realise this wasn't just *any* Sally; *this was my Sally*. It was Dakota.

My head felt tighter; heat flushed through my body, my stomach felt weird, and it wasn't because of the Skittles.

"Dakota?" I managed to blurt out unexpectedly.

She turned around, her green eyes widened, and she froze. My jaw felt hard as I pressed my teeth together.

I heard Jamie say, 'Oh, bollocks." Jamie was, of course, Jack Skellington.

"Augusta?" Dakota spluttered. "Wh..Wh...What are you doing here?"

Me? I felt like I was about to explode.

"What's going on? What are YOU doing here?" I raged back.

Dakota stepped forward, "I didn't know how to tell you. I got invited to this party, and I've never been to one on Halloween before and...."

Jamie stepped forward too. "It's my fault, Augusta," he interrupted. "I wanted to come, and I begged D to come with me. It's our first Halloween together. You can understand that, can't you?"

ARE YOU KIDDING ME!!! ALL I HAVE DONE IS BE BLOODY UNDERSTANDING!!!

I didn't want to pay any attention to him. Since he's come onto the scene, Dakota has been a completely different person. He's changed her, and not for the better.

Instead, I focused on her. "Why didn't you just tell me you wanted to go to this stupid party? Why lie to me? I thought we were friends!?!"

"I didn't think you'd understand, and I didn't want to upset you. I..."

Before Dakota could finish whatever, she was saying, I heard Johanna's voice. I looked to where the noise came from and saw they were all there! I was the only one in this so-called gang who wasn't worth an invite! All the entitled elitist, arrogant snobs were in a big circle like I was the main event at a public execution.

What has happened to my friend? Why does she want this? Be a part of *this*? When did our friendship become so bloody mediocre and tedious that it wasn't worth any honesty?

I saw Zayn. He and Tucker were Lock and Barrell from Nightmare before Christmas. I guess they, Jamie and Dakota came as a group. Johanna, Renee, and Tamara were all practically wearing underwear. I don't even know who they were supposed to be.

"What's going on?" Johanna said. "You guys coming? Why are you all out here?"

Johanna looked at me like I came straight from a sewer pipe. "Who invited her? Is that your costume? Hoodie and Jeans?" She leant in my direction as she spoke. Her top lip curled in disgust. "*Who* are you meant to be exactly?"

Jamie held his hand up toward her. His eyes concentrated on me. "In a minute, Johanna. Please go back in. We'll meet you there in a bit."

I was surrounded. The untouchables were all staring at me, gawking, waiting for drama, enjoying the show.

We were on two sides. The crowd stood shoulder to shoulder, like an army against an intruder. I stood deserted.

Theirs was a world I could only watch and never belong. I was the odd one out, the weirdo, a different being, an unworthy candidate for their attention. How did I get to this? Why am I constantly on my own with no one to stand beside me? Why is it always me against them? Why me? Why?

I couldn't help letting out a snivelling sob, as I spoke directly to Dakota. "Why don't you want to be my friend anymore? Why don't you want to be with me? WHY DON'T YOU CARE!?!"

Dakota was silent, but I could hear the crowd.

"Bloody hell Augusta, calm down.", "Fugly's getting a bit miffed.", "Blimey, she's even more fugly now!"

I could feel my body tense and burning. Dakota needed to speak. Why wasn't she saying anything? Doesn't she owe me at least that? "ANSWER ME, DAKOTA! NOW! WHY DON'T YOU CARE?"

"What the hell's wrong with you? Are you in love with her or something?" "Watch out, J, competition!" "I'm bored."

I blocked out the crowd and fixated on Dakota. Tears streamed down her face. Jamie had his arm around her and spoke softly to me. "Augusta, let's go somewhere and talk, okay?"

"J? What about the party?" It was Luca. I didn't even notice he was there before, to be honest. Luca was dressed as Edward Scissorhands, and Rosie beside him was Kim. I guess they didn't get the message about The Nightmare before Christmas.

"Luca, it doesn't matter," Jamie answered. Dakota kept her eyes on me.

Rosie came toward me. "Augusta, do you want to come with me? She had her hand outstretched.

I looked at them all, taking in the scene. I was being handled like a wild animal needing to be tamed so it could return to its cage. They looked at me with pity. All crowded around like I was an annoying problem they had to work together to solve. All of this fake concern, none of them cared or wanted me there. They needed me to go away so they could drink vodka and party.

I had become an inconvenience, irritating them, and stopping them from enjoying their night. They were getting drunk in a big fancy house, in their silly costumes, acting as if they were God's gift and desired by everyone. The irony is that I didn't want to be there either. So why was I?

Upon this realisation, I did the smart thing and stepped back. A few called my name, but I turned and ran away. I kept running until exhaustion hit, and I no longer had the energy to feel angry.

I came to a bus stop, sat down, and vacantly existed.

Deprived of any sensation.

I spaced out.

Confused.

Impassive.

I don't know how long I was there before I noticed her. But, of course, it would be her. The girl's timing is impeccable. Thai was in a Sally costume too.

She looked over and said, "hey." Her hair was thick and long; you couldn't tell it was a wig. The dress fitted around her body perfectly.

Of course, she looked exquisite. She always does. "Not a good night to be alone."

I looked at her as she spoke to me. Thai was smiling. What would it be like to touch her? To have her touching me? I needed to feel arms around me, know someone wanted me there. Her mouth seemed to be waiting. Longing for contact.

I smiled at her; I was grateful she was there. Her face softened. Thai was looking at me too. It felt like a moment, it felt right, so I leaned in and kissed her.

After all the times I was so infatuated with her, I dreamed about what it would be like. But after so many scenarios in my head, I felt absolutely nothing.

"Oh my God! What is wrong with you! You are so weird. No wonder no one wants to be around you! Go home, you freak! Oh right, they don't want you there either. You don't belong anywhere, do you? Why are you here? Go away, Augusta, do everyone a favour, and go away! Eliminate yourself."

So, I ran home.

Alone, rejected, unwanted.

Mum and Mac were cuddled on the sofa, enjoying their time together.

I went up to my bed, and I knew.

It was time for this persecution to stop. I can't do this anymore.

I force myself through every insufferable day- no one knows how hard it is to get out of bed. To walk to school, knowing what is coming; enduring class after class, relentless daily pressure to be 'alright' so no one feels awkward. Everyone wants me to smile, to be happy, always telling me, 'Cheer up, Augusta'.

I can't remember the last time I truly was cheerful. Or the last time I giggled, roared with laughter, or even felt content.

Isn't it my fundamental human right to feel safe, not suffer agony and despair?

I try, but I fail. I'm a failure. I don't fit.

They tell me, 'Try harder, 'work harder, 'be better.
But I say No.
No more.
Nothing I do is ever right or good enough. I am deformed, broken, loathsome. Disgusting Augusta.

I'm forever climbing a sand dune in the dark. I want to get to the top, but I'm going sideways across the desert- an infinite mass of setbacks and hardship. The weight of purely existing is gruelling and murderous. There is no end to this, so it is down to me to create one.

I have nothing left to offer and nothing left to give. I am done.

I decide on Thursday, November 5th.

There is no other way. I can feel my heart beating in my throat as if it's already trying to get away. In a few days, it will get its wish.

I have no energy.
I only need enough clothes for 4 more days, so I put all the rest in bin bags and ask Mac to donate them to children in Africa. He looked a bit bewildered. So, I told him I was getting rid of clothes that didn't fit me and were more suited for the summer. He shrugged and put them in the garage.

I worked through all my possessions and made a list of anything important, so it will go to people I trust and love. I put all of them underneath my bed, so the special things were together. I put the list with the name beside it in an envelope ready for Thursday (November 5th).

I want my art stuff to go to Rosie. Although I don't know her all that well, she has been nice to me and loves art. I don't think she knows how it feels to be around someone you know will be kind, because it's in their nature. Rosie was always genuine. I relaxed around her, and we had good conversations. that means the world to someone like me, and she helped me a lot when I tried to get to know Jamie. Rosie makes people feel she cares.
I've been working on some pieces of art to leave behind. It means a lot to me that people know it's not their fault. I need them to see the pain and heartbreak I have inside.

I want the people closest to me to have a piece of me, something completely unique that can't be replaced. I'm not saying they would miss me, but it might bring them comfort if they ever feel sad.

I made one for Dakota. It was a silhouette of two

young girls holding hands outside a circus
tent in the moonlight. 'This is Us' is written
above it in stars. Tiny shooting stars
surround it.

        For Dad, I drew a picture of him holding me as a
baby. I think that was the time he most enjoyed being my
father. We are staring into each other's eyes, and I am
holding onto his finger with my whole fist. I need Dad to
know I loved him and was always his baby girl. We got lost
past a simpler age when he had all the answers and knew
how he could protect me.
        Mac. My favourite thing about him is his smile. Mac's
whole face lights up, and his joy is projected like a sunbeam
to all those around him.
        I want Mac to be happy. So, I drew his family he can
now have, Mum and two little kids. A boy and a girl, each
with his magical smile, dark skin, and a mass of curly hair;
the girl has hers in bunches. Mac is bald but told me once
he has to shave his head otherwise, he'd be sporting this big
ass afro that would look like it could take over the world.
So, his children would definitely have thick black curly hair.
The kids have Mum's eyes, and in front of each of them is a
plate with a stack of pancakes.
And the picture for Mum. I did a painting. She knows I
hardly do any as I prefer charcoal and sketching, so it
made it special.
        The artwork is of her and me. A dazzling heart is
between us to represent the amount of love she has
bestowed upon me. I always felt it.

We are both smiling but surrounded by black clouds. My older self is in the background, high amongst the storm; I have lines on my face and am in more boring grown-up clothes. The future me is faint against the darkness. I wrote my favourite memories we shared on the back of each gift:

My Dad was, of course, my 10th birthday party, us away with the fairies. I told him how much it meant to me for him to go to so much effort. How unreal it felt to ride a real unicorn, how magical to meet and play with Tinkerbell, and to have friends all around me. I cherish that day. He loved me so much that he made all my dreams come true.

For Mac, it was every Christmas he has lived with us. He always tries to make Christmas special. The lounge is filled with the angelic sound of carols and a bonfire showing on TV to give an illusion of a homely atmosphere. He makes Christmas pancakes for breakfast, colouring the batter red and green. He decorates them with tons of berries and lashings of cinnamon cream.

Mum has never liked turkey, so he does a wellington of venison, salmon, or beef instead, and cooks the best roast potatoes. After a walk, we would arrive back home, and he'd give us a slice of his homemade yule log with Cornish clotted cream. Mac has always wanted to please us. And I mean us, not just Mum. He would write me a letter inside my Christmas card detailing all his favourite moments with me from the past year. For Mac, Christmas is a time to show love and be thankful for each other. At Christmas, he always makes me appreciate how thankful I am for him.

For Dakota, I told her she meant everything.

I don't have to think of any poignant moments because I am thankful for every minute we have spent together. She is my best friend. I know it hasn't been easy for her to have me as hers, but I will always be grateful.

It was the simple things like having a laugh and people-watching on the bench in town. We sang 'A million dreams' at the top of our voices and performed together at the school play. Every time we watched Jack Skellington discover Christmas and bring it to Halloween town. We smuggled Oreos into school camp and took selfies with black bits in our teeth. One time we tried walking across a log, we both fell into the river- my mind is littered with so many moments that seem tiny and insignificant but hold so much value when I reminisce on dark days.

I told her, I don't know if you felt you had to change to fit in more with Jamie and his friends, but in case you did- I think you are perfect as you are. I always have. You told me Jamie liked you before the straighteners and gorgeous hair at the start of term, so I think he thinks of you that way too. So, Dakota please believe in yourself and start to see how we see you.

My last memory was the hardest. Mum.

The truth is I had so many. But I chose something Mum might not expect.

I wrote. Mum, When you broke up our family, I didn't understand. It had always been you, Dad, and me, my whole life; I always assumed it would always be that way. Us against the world. But your revelation that night shattered everything and seemed to come out of nowhere. I was angry; you and Dad were angry too.

My Dad became miserable overnight. You were always crying; I kept thinking, why put everyone through this? So, I decided to try and help. I did chores to stop extra stress and anger and gave you extra hugs. I tried to reassure you, "Don't worry, you can take it back; Dad will forgive you."

I was selfish. I only saw things from my point of view. As I got older, I began to look at things differently. I thought about how your life was secure, safe, and had a path and future all laid out.

I was happy and content, so was Dad, but no one was thinking about you. You weren't in love anymore. You naturally and instinctively put everyone else first, and it occurred to me how brave you had to be to make a stand for yourself. Knowing you would hurt the two people you cared about more than anyone. How they might never forgive you for ruining the illusion that our lives were perfect.

But Mum, there was nothing to forgive. You were right to be courageous, give yourself a chance to lead your best life, and become a better person. I cherish the memories we had as a family and the ones we make together now.

You get to do what so many people wish they could- live without regret. To use your words, I am in awe of you. I want to be courageous. I want to be brave and be more like you. I know that's what you want too, but I'm afraid I must let you down.

I am thankful for every minute we spent together, Mum, good or bad (I know, I nicked your line again, but it was a good one).

You inspire me. You make so many things better; I love you so much. And I am so proud of you for taking control of your life. I hope you can understand one day why I had to take control of mine.

I lay on my bed, both mentally and physically exhausted. I can't believe it's school tomorrow. I only have to make it through three more days of school, as well as Thursday, Then, I can relax because it will soon be over.

printed it out in Mac's office and stuck them in instead.

Hi, It's J.
D is really upset.
Look, it wasn't her fault, she didn't know what to do. D really wanted 2 go to the party with me but she also didn't want to let u down- especially after you reached out (thanx for doing that btw).
I made her go to the party and told D she could rearrange coming to yours. It was bad of me, and I'm sorry
Telling u she was poorly was also my idea, so if u wanna hate or be mad aim that at me. D cares about u so much.
I hate seeing her like this and being the reason u r apart, and not speaking. We both feel so bad.
Again, I'm sorry. Spk soon x J

Hey, Augusta,
I wanted to check you were ok. I was a bit worried about you after last night.
If you want to chat or anything, let me know x
We can hang out, maybe go to an art gallery, or exhibition or something? Luca hates all that stuff, but it might be quite cool. Let me know,
Hope everything's alright,
Lots of love Rosie xxxx

Hey, it's me. I'm so sorry I lied. I'm sorry I've been such a rubbish friend to you. I lied because I thought it would be kinder as I didn't want you to think I didn't want to be with you. Sounds stupid I know. I thought we could watch movies anytime, and the party was that one night. I've never been invited to a party before- obviously as a kid, but not a proper one with a boyfriend. I know I was selfish and I didn't think of you.
The costumes were ba surprise from J. He knows how much I love the film and he said tucker and zayn wanted in on it too. He surprised me with them that night and I started crying straightaway cause I felt so guiklty. Not only did I lie to you but with one of our favourite films. He didn't know it was our thing, he was only trying to be thoughtful.
I know you are angery and hurt but pleasr forgive me so we can be friends again. I will always think of you as my best friend. X xx

I only replied to Dakota. This is what I sent:

> In four days I will be gone. You have new friends now. Enjoy them and your boyfriend. Have a nice life.

Dakota answered with just one word: 'Ok.'

I felt strangely desolate. It's like we are done and said goodbye. Our time together was over. I guess it doesn't matter to her if I am living or dead. Eventually, I couldn't think or feel anymore, so I went to bed.

It's 3am, and I'm not sleeping again. Instead, I'm lying here thinking of conversations and parts of the last few days I wish I could erase. Halloween, the kiss, the messages I sent. I want to change things, but I'm scared.

Today was okay. But I had PE, which I hate.

My Mum gave me a note to excuse myself after what happened on her birthday, but now my cuts have healed, and she's noticed, so no more notes. She said if I'm on report, I must try to make an effort. Today was hard as I haven't done any exercise for a couple weeks. My body thanked me with multiple stitches in my tummy and I had no sympathy from Mr Farthing or Miss Fry, my PE teachers.

I didn't go to French or History- why put myself through it? I didn't want to sit next to Dakota, and just the thought of French class and dealing with Jenna Dawson is horrifying.

So, I went into town and walked around Elizabeth Gardens instead. The gardens are a nice little space with statues dedicated to war veterans. So, I guess I did get a touch of history, after all. I read the inscriptions. I wondered what they thought, being so young, knowing they were about to die. Were they scared?

How many died alone? Not many, I expect. But they had to see things that scarred them. It's awful that you could be so hated for who you are, where you are from. The most moving bits of war footage I have seen is when soldiers help each other when they are from opposite sides. They aren't supposed to be nice to one another; everyone expects them to hate. But instead, they don't listen to the masses and show kindness. I could see Zayn in a few statues and wondered if I lived in a simpler time, would I have survived? I can hope.

When I was little, I thought Elizabeth Gardens were massive, but it's tiny. Pretty though.

In Ethics, Jamie and Zayn tried saying hello, but I pretended I didn't hear and walked away. I didn't want to speak to either of them.

I didn't write yesterday; I got through school and did some art. I saw Dakota in Science, and straight off, she asked me, "What did you mean when you said you'd be gone? Are you moving away, or changing schools or something?"

"No, Dakota," I answered. "I plan to die."

"That's not funny, Augusta."

I looked her straight in the eyes and said, "No, it isn't." Immediately afterward, I walked out the door.

I couldn't be around her, so she could ask me stupid questions after making it obvious how little she cared. I hadn't unpacked my schoolbag, so I grabbed it and went. I could hear my teacher calling my name, but I kept going because I already recognised the signs. My breathing had quickened, and the fear was setting in. I knew I was having a panic attack.

I walked to the side of the science block, crouched down, and lay on the floor, trying to breathe. My chest tightened, and I felt pain. Maybe it was a heart attack. I curled up into a ball on the cold stone floor and closed my eyes.

I prayed silently in my head, 'please, not like this, please.' I didn't want to die on concrete. I melted into the ground and repeated my prayer.

Early last night, Mac came into my room before Mum got home. The first thing he said was how tidy it was. I thought this was a strange thing to say as I had my art sketches sprawled over my bed.

"Where's all your stuff?" he asked me.

"Tidied away," I said.

"I had a call from your dad. The school phoned him- said you walked out in Science."

"I had a panic attack."

"A bad one?"

"Yes." I snapped. I didn't mean to, but I could hardly say I was spread on the floor and ended up with grit all over me and in my hair.

He looked tired. "Are you okay? You've spent a lot of time in your room lately. We miss you."

I half smiled and nodded- hoping it was enough. It wasn't.

"You can talk to me, you know."

"I know."

Mac leaned against my wall. "Boy trouble?"

Good grief.

His eyebrows raised, "girl trouble?"

Thai. Without thinking, I looked at him, I quickly looked down at my drawing, but I was too slow. I obviously gave something away.

"You know nobody knows at your age. And I don't mean that condescendingly. Most people are confused with feelings for girls and boys well into their twenties. It happens more than you think."

I *really* didn't want to talk about this. Why was Mac here? Why can't he go back to work and leave me alone?

But he was determined to have his say. "I mean, even I experimented when I was younger."

Ground swallow me whole now.

"My best friend and his girl. We ya know...."

I did not know, and I do not want to know. Please stop right there. Why would you tell me what you did with your best friend and his girlfriend? I don't even know how that would even work!

He smiled at me. "We did stuff. And you know it did feel good."

Ew.

"I can tell you're uncomfortable," Mac laughed. "Don't worry too much about labels, okay? You already got one- Augusta Walsh. If the world's population lived solely on labels, we would run out pretty damn quick. People are complicated. It's okay not to know, okay?"

Please stop talking.

I humoured him. "Thanks, Mac."

"No problem."

The poor man thinks he's helped.

"Mum might be late from the hospital. How about I treat us to some fish and chips?"

"I'm not hungry, Mac, to be honest."

"No problem. I probably need to cut down anyway." He patted his flat-toned stomach.

Thankfully, he decided he tortured me enough and was gone.

Today I told Chloe and Jennifer thank you for helping me and taking charge of all the stuff in Drama. They said, "It's okay. That's what's friends are for."

It made me think maybe I should have hung out with them more. I wonder if Jennifer and Chloe feel like I used them.

Jennifer seems better after the whole Dominic thing. A bit more like herself, the school moved on to a new victim. But I should have checked up on her more and stood up for her. I feel bad I didn't. Do they think I am a good friend? Probably not. Or maybe we came together as a group because we don't belong anywhere else.

For me, the last day of school was much like my life-uneventful. No one asked me if anything was happening, there were no tearful goodbyes, no one asked, "isn't tonight the night you plan to kill yourself?"

They carried on with their lives happily, utterly oblivious to anyone else.

I tried writing my own tombstone.

Here lies Augusta Walsh

Age 15 years, 4 months, and 6 days

Daughter, Friend, Granddaughter

Disconsolation is no longer home

I want a black one, I think it would be fitting. I found the word 'disconsolation' after searching on Google. It comes from 'disconsolate' and means cheerless, gloomy, beyond consolation (consoling somebody, easing their pain). I think it shows there was no answer to how to make things any better. It says what I had to do and why, without it being in your face, which at a graveyard somehow seems inappropriate or disrespectful. As an only child, I have no nieces and nephews yet to be born or descendants coming to visit and putting flowers on my grave. But for Mum, Dad, and Mac, it seems a good way of reminding them that things were too much and there was no way out. None I can think of anyway.

I had a last meal with Mum and Mac, and again, it was depressingly ordinary. Chicken nuggets, chips, and broccoli. The most boring vegetable there is. Mum told me off because I left loads and kept moving my food around the plate.

I came upstairs and called Dad. There were lots of awkward silences, which was a bit disappointing. As usual, he didn't know what to say to me, apart from asking about school. I said it was fine. Afterwards, he began talking about Mum, which was annoying, so I said, "I got to go."

He didn't want to know if I was free or what I was doing, which would have been an opener to confide to him about my plans. But I guess he doesn't care.

I had a dream last night.

I was in this field, and around me were these mini trees that only came to my shoulder. They were beautiful. The sun shone in a clear blue sky and lit them all up. I could see their skeletons shining through. There were so many colours, even ones that leaves shouldn't be, like purple and blue. On the outskirts of the field were regular tall trees flourishing in a beautiful spectrum.

In this dream, I remembered my science lesson at school and how imperfect every leaf was. Yet here they were, magnificently majestic and enchanting. How could something so abnormal and mutated be this spectacular? I felt at home, safe. I was exactly where I belonged. It was heavenly and celestial; and for once, I wasn't alone.

Within this nature's kaleidoscope at the top of the field were Dakota, Jamie, Rosie, Luca, Zayn, Jennifer, and Chloe. They were all waiting for me wearing white.

I moved smoothly, feeling the leaves with my fingertips as I let my arms fall. They did not feel rough or crisp; instead, the leaves felt like my suede Dr Marten boots that I used to love before I grew out of them.

I approached my friends, and they parted to show me a tree tunnel. I looked through, and it led into a cold cave. Jagged pointy rocks curved above a dark, murky river, where a worn, rickety boat was waiting for me. I looked at the cloudless bright blue sky and the bleak black tunnel.

I pleaded, begged my friends not to make me go into melancholy. I don't want to leave and be alone, lost in the dark. The rocks and sea looked so gloomy and cold. I wanted warmth, belonging, and affection. I knelt and prayed for help, but no one was listening. I was on my own even though surrounded by people I knew.

I opened my mouth to scream for help, and no sound came. Clouds covered the light, the sun became cold, and the leaves, trees and my fairy-tale field shrivelled up and became strokes of charcoal.

Nothing was left for me. My friends remained there, and the sun's light seemed to channel solely onto them, making them glow in luminous golden energy.

I made my way through the tunnel of trees. I had no oar; I had to use my hand to move the boat. The water was thick, sluggish. I looked back and saw my friends watching me, each one glowing like a beacon, but I did not know if I could reach out.

I felt water beneath my feet. The boat was sinking and went under. The water pulled me down to the sullied seabed. I was drowning, and the only person who could save me was me.

I decided to send one last message to Dakota, Chloe, and Rosie. I used WhatsApp

> I can't do this anymore.
> Everything is too hard. I don't want to be here.
> In a few hours I will be gone (I know you may want me to live, but I am not good at it, I don't know how). It's so much work and I need it all to end.
> Goodbye. Thank you for being my friend.
> Augusta.

I'll write again when it is time.

Thursday 5th November
Augusta Walsh
Age 15 years, 4 months, and 6 days.
Time: 7:05pm

Nobody is here. Only me.

Colours flash at my window, screeches, and popping. Yet nobody is out there, no messages, no matter how many times I check. No one has answered, no ticks turning blue to say I have been seen, no one wants to know how I'm doing, to say hello, or start any conversation with me.

Nobody wants to be with me again. I am alone.

People are busy living and having fun with their real friends, those they care about and love. I have no one trying to offer me another way or help me think of a different solution. Not one has read my message. Not a single person cares.

I can't reach out again and force myself into their world.

I just reread it. I sound so stupid and presumptuous. *'I know you may want me to live'*, I don't know that at all. They might have been hoping, waiting for me to come to my senses. I put my phone on silent and removed the notifications so I could ignore them back. I don't want to know anymore; I want to shut everyone out. Why don't they care about me? What's wrong with me?

I curl up in my duvet; I feel small. My body is weighed down like it's not mine to manipulate or move. All I have is this notebook and pen. I checked, and again no messages. All I have is you. I have given everything else away. After I'm gone, people will find this notebook and hopefully know that you don't have to be older to experience real suffering and pain.

I relented and put my phone notifications back on and the volume up.

I hate this blank screen. I am so sad and lonely; I wish I was Thai. I would have been more loved, more likeable, and had what I needed most of all. A mate. One mate I could tell my worries and thoughts to, that wasn't this book. Someone who wouldn't judge me or make me feel like a burden, and affection wouldn't be forced. Instead, we would openly say we loved each other, tell the whole world, go bowling, treat ourselves to Starbucks and surf.

I tried hard to be happy, but it was so much pressure. No one can be happy the whole damn time. Sometimes the darkness and fear of this being the only thing there is, overwhelms me. I want to experience how to do more than merely survive. I want to know how I can live. I crave it. To feel alive, but I cannot live this life.

I exist day after day, trying to be the person everyone else wants and needs me to be. I am a failure at being normal. I wish I could be true to myself, but I don't know who that is yet. I'm still learning but also struggling. I need help. Who can help me?

I rechecked. No blue ticks.

My mum has been asking about my 16th. She mentioned it again at teatime, I wanted to say it was pointless even talking about it, but I wasn't courageous enough.

Imagine if I kept existing till then. How would it work? Mum, Mac, and Dad with Gran at a restaurant- it would kill my dad seeing Mum and Mac for that length of time together. He would drink himself into a stupor.

A party? Invite who? I have no friends. No one would care enough to turn up. There are no options for me.

It's time. This will be the last time I write.

My chair is in position.

I lift my wooden jewellery box and put it on my bed. I have no jewellery in there apart from a small charm bracelet and a signet ring that belonged to my grandfather. I never wear necklaces, bracelets, or rings, so it's photos and little memento bits. Captured memories of me with Mum and Dad, Me and Dakota, my Gran as a young woman, the gold embossed invitation and map to my fairy 10th birthday party, my first concert seeing Billie Ellish with my Aunty Lou. My first day of school, Mum and Dad's wedding.

There's a great picture of Mum and me on the beach laughing on the sand. It looks like a nice day, and we look so happy. It was strange seeing myself smiling. I remember that day, being carefree and enjoying the sun.

There's a card from my Gold Class primary teacher telling me I'm special and always aim for the stars.

It warms my heart to look through these little keepsakes. I enjoyed being alive, I used to laugh, I used to do things, have a reason to remember a special day, when did I forget how? When did I become so unlovable no one wanted to snap a picture, enable a way to remember our time together? I grieve for that girl. I want her back. When will the world look beneath my mask, see through my act to notice how broken I truly am?

Everyone has witnessed my amateur performance; I have always hidden in plain sight. Why has no one looked closer? Told me, "I see you're not okay. Let's talk."

I leave the box on my bed, so they know I loved them and were in my final thoughts when I'm found.

I go to my drawer and take out the art I'd been hiding. It's important they know why. This is how I feel. It will help them understand the darkness that submerges my thoughts and invade my head. I am a cannibal of my own self. If I don't do something, there will not be any of the old Augusta, that little fairy girl on the beach, left to remember.

I am scared, so scared. I wish there was another way out. How can a body live on when all my mind wants to do is relent and fade to dust?

Still no messages, still no blue ticks.

I don't know what will happen, but I can't see a way out. I need to believe in some kind of light, a hope I can head toward. I wear a mask every day. Inside, the tears have never stopped flowing. I am tired of being this peculiar involuntary recluse trapped within a solitary life. I need someone to carry the load for a while, so I'm not always shattered. I am completely knackered 24/7.

I wish someone would love me when they had a choice whether they have to. Although Mum, Dad, and Mac do, I have no friends to say, "It will be okay, I'm here."

No blue ticks.

I guess this proves everyone will be fine. No more Augusta the liability, the dysfunctional freak they have to tiptoe around who ruins everything. They will be finally free.

I pick up the picture of Mum and me at the beach. This is the Augusta everyone wants. This Augusta would go surfing, have a job so she could ski in Italy, have big plans for her 16th, this Augusta would be getting excellent grades, have her own style, her plan for life. But most of all, she would be bright, joyful, and light-hearted. There would be no mask- her smile would be genuine, her laugh would be natural, and everyone would know everything was okay and there was a great future. She would know that too.

I wish I was back to when things were simpler. I looked at my bedroom door, waiting for a knock. Someone to check on me. But there is silence, only a faint murmur from the television downstairs. No one is coming.

Knock, please.

Nothing.

I will always struggle with my own head. I've never even been kissed properly. I am going to die having never felt that intimacy with another person. I know everyone else has, but the opportunity never came for me, and I was never fearless enough to create it.

I guess it's fitting my final minutes are spent in quietness. I always thought if I spoke out loud about the darkness, people would call me insane. But I constantly feel the urge to scream. So, instead, I tell them nothing, so I don't force them to walk away.

I have done the last drawing, my final image. It's of me smiling like I am at the beach, but I am small, almost hidden in the corner. In the main bit, there is a group of people. They are smiling, laughing, and looking in wonder at the fireworks in the sky. As always, they are out of reach, enjoying themselves. I can't get there. I use different colours for the sky and make it beautiful.

My phone is blank and cold. I look at my door and listen. The only noise comes from my window as bangs and cackles entertaining the lucky ones. Outside is lit up, reminding me I am an imposter. An intruder trespassing in a disarming, illuminated, daunting, intimidating world. I am stuck in a rabbit hole, searching for a crumb so I can grow and find a way out.

No blue ticks. I can no longer do this. Everything must end. I catch my breath and stand up.

Soon my last breath. I don't want to do this. I'm terrified.

My face is wet from tears, my nose is running. I wipe it with my sleeve. I take the beach photo and put it in the pocket of my jeans.

I love you, Mum. You are with me. I look at my door. Still nothing.

Final check on my phone. Nothing.

It is time to say goodbye.

My phone beeped.

It was Dakota.

I love you. I'm coming over now. I'll be there in 15.

Straight after her message, a knock came on my door.

Weightlessness, I started to breathe.

Sunday December 28
Augusta Walsh
Age 25, 5 months, and 28 days.

I found this notebook in my Mum's garage when looking through some boxes of my old stuff. Reading through it brought everything back, and it was actually really emotional. It's awful when you feel as trapped as I did. You can't see a way out or imagine things getting any better. Luckily for me, that knock was Mum and Mac; they found me sobbing. My whole body sunk into the chair as soon as I knew help was coming. Mum held me that night for the longest time.

Dakota arrived with Jamie straight after, and that night I opened up. They sat around in this circle, each holding onto me so I could feel their love and support. Mum called Dad over too. I told them everything I could, but I was so exhausted. Chloe and Rosie visited me that weekend, so my support network grew. Over the next few days, I continued to talk and found I had many more friends to confide in than I realised.

I think speaking out saved me. Sending that message on WhatsApp to my friends was the best thing I could have done. Dakota rang Mum as soon she saw it.
After a lot of therapy and trust in my family and friends, I slowly healed. Depression still rears its ugly head every now and again, but I have strategies now. All those problems I had, it felt like they would continue mounting. But it DOES end. School life doesn't last forever. Eventually, life gets easier because you get older and learn how to handle things in a better way.

I went to college, followed by university, and completed my degree with honours a couple years ago. Now I work as a photographer and have my own business with my partner. I still see Dakota; we remain best friends to this day. And she and Jamie are still together. I hear about Luca and Zayn through them. They both work trade jobs now, and each has a couple of kids.

Rosie and I mostly keep in touch through social media. She is a teacher for a primary school in Scotland and loves her life. Chloe is in London, trying to be an actress. She's been in a few things but pretty small-time. Chloe wants to work in the West End eventually, and I have no doubt she'll be on centre stage singing and dancing before she knows it. Jennifer works for a magazine and lives in New Zealand. She is incredibly happy, married and expecting her first baby.

I haven't seen Johanna in years, but Dakota told me she works in a fast-food restaurant and looks completely opposite to when she was at school.

Dad is in his own home now. I took over the mortgage, and I'm selling the house to move close to the beach. I found my perfect home; I'll get to see the sea every day. Dad and I have a better relationship now than back then. He hasn't been drinking for years, and he's really happy with a lovely lady called Jane. Dad brightens up every time he sees her. They got married last year.

Mum and Mac live in a big house with their little boy, Wesley. But everyone calls him Wes. He's got Mac's smile; I adore him. Mum and Mac never married; they never saw the need, but they are great together.

I did do something for my 16th birthday. Mum and Mac took me, Dakota, and Chloe for a weekend in Dublin. Not quite skiing in Italy, but we had a blast, and there were many enchanting fairy-tale castles for us to explore.

I guess I'm writing this for my 15-year-old self. I wanted to show that even at her darkest moment, she was strong and courageous, and in the end, like in the dream, she saved herself. She found a way out and did it all at rock bottom. Amazing Augusta.

I wish I could speak to her now, I would love to tell her; I got to pursue our dream, to use our artistic ability to build our future. But you had the one element inside of you that we needed most of all. Bravery. Mum was right. You were spectacular.

I smile every day. Genuinely. And I laugh until my stomach aches and make other people laugh too. Importantly, I travelled. I got on a plane and saw the world, including Italy.

So, thank you, 15-year-old Augusta. Because you spoke out, because you reached out to your friends, you saved our lives. Thanks to you, we not only got to feel alive. We got to live.

The future is unwritten

Dear Reader

If you are struggling and would like some advice and support, there are many free, confidential ways to get help online and beyond. Whatever you are going through, you don't have to face it alone.

Childline,

The Childline number is 0800 1111, it's free and confidential and is open 24 hours a day, seven days a week. Children and young people can also use a one-to-one chat service on the website and send emails to counsellors via their Childline lockers on their accounts. Additionally, there are message boards on the website, where young people can seek peer support with their worries, this is a moderated and safe space and many children have told us it's a great place to seek initial validation for their worries and it has inspired them to look for further help.

There is also a Calm Zone on the website www.childline.org.uk which is a dedicated space for helping children and young people with mental health and their worries.

The Samaritans

When life is difficult, Samaritans are here – day or night, 365 days a year. You can call them for free on 116 123, email them at jo@samaritans.org, or visit www.samaritans.org for more information.

Stem4

Stem4 is a charity that promotes positive mental health in teenagers and those who support them including their families and carers. The website has a mass amount including a library of free mental health resources.
stem4.org.uk

Apps
Calm Harm - a free app to help young people manage the urge to self-harm

Clear Fear - a free app to help children & young people manage the symptoms of anxiety

Combined Minds - a free app to help families & friends provide mental health support for teenagers

Mood Move - a free app to help with low mood and depression

stem4 apps - Calm Harm, Clear Fear, Combined Minds, Move Mood

If an adult or parent is worried about the welfare of a child or their child, they can call the NSPCC helpline for advice on 0808 800 5000 or email help@nspcc.org.uk. Our helpline isn't just for reporting abuse, it's for advice for adults too.

Acknowledgements

Young mental health is an increasingly important issue that is underrepresented in literature, particularly fiction. I hoped to portray a modern-day teenager with real problems that people could relate to. We must continue to shine a light on this subject and keep talking.

I wish to thank all the teenagers who opened up about their anxiety and fears, helping me understand enough to try and accurately represent your demographic. Hopefully, you feel I did a good enough job.
Thank you for taking the time to teach me and show me what matters most to you.

To Eliza, thank you for all your hard work, beautiful art, and expressing Augusta in such a vivid and creative way. I look at your craft and am constantly blown away by your natural talent and dedication. I am proud to have you work with me on this project.

To Gavin, thank you for being amazingly patient while I explored teenage life and worked toward those deadlines. Your endless support for my work as an author is unparalleled. I will forever be grateful.

To Archie, Eliza, and Hugo, I'm always here, listening with my arms and mind open. I love you more than salt.

Thank you, Stem4, NSPCC, and the Samaritans, for all your help and support. Your work is beyond the scope of remarkable. On behalf of the world, we thank you.

To my advance readers; Olivia Griggs, Cordelia Smith, Liza Radmore, Caitlin Reel, Lilia Tofts, Oscar Manlove, Ava Mallett, Evie Hutchenson, Rhianna Heasman, Harmony Heasman, Amber Carver, and Lexi D. Thank you for agreeing to take a chance on me, donate your time, and support a local author. Jim Rohn said, 'Reading is essential for those who seek to rise above the ordinary.' You are already extraordinary in my eyes. Thank you.

And finally, to you, my reader. Thank you for taking the time to read this book. My aim was simple when I first began this project; I wanted to show that you are not alone. In thoughts you may have, your feelings, your worries, I wanted you to be aware that others have them too.
Speak to a friend, use the helplines in the back of this book, and download those apps because, and this is essential you understand this: You are important.
There is only one of you in the entire history of life on earth. Only one human has existed that looks precisely like you; thinks or acts like you. This means you are already the most perfect version of yourself. The best ever. Show the world how special you are. The universe is waiting.

Bibliography

Can I tell you about Depression?
Christopher Dowrick and Susan Martin
Jessica Kingsley　　ISBN: 978-1849055635

Blame my Brain, Nicola Morgan
Walker Books　ISBN: 978-1-4063-0

The teenage guide to Stress, Nicola Morgan
Walker Books　ISMB: 978-1-4063-5314-3

NHS Mental Health of Children and Young People in England
Survey 2021　Publication Date: 30th September 2021

Mental ill-health among children of the new century trends across
childhood with a focus on age 14; Patalay P & Fitzsimons E
September 2017, Centre for Longitudal Studies, London.

Am I depressed and what can I do about it?
Shirley Reynolds and Monika Parkinson
Robinson　　ISBN: 978-1-4721-1453-2

The Human Mind, Professor Robert Winston
　　　　　Bantam Press　ISBN: 978-0593052105

About the Author

Melanie Stephens is a full-time author of fiction. She published her first book, Isolation Tales in 2020 as a way to help raise money for the NHS. It featured fictional stories and poems, highlighting the work of keyworkers during the pandemic. Her story attracted both national and local press, and her book received five-str rave reviews.

In 2022, Isolation Tales joined the Cornish archive at Kresen Kernow, the World's largest collection of documents, book, maps and photographs relating to Cornwall's history. The Collection, her second book showcased her writing journey so far, and again attracted five-star reviews.

You can find out more, and updates about Melanie's work at www.melaniestephensauthor.com and follow her on Facebook, Instagram and via the blog: https://geekgirleatscake.home.blog/

 # GET IN TOUCH

I have an email address just for readers which you can get in touch with me on. Whether you want to talk about a book, writing, cups of tea, pasties, or to say hi- I'm listening!

Every email comes directly to me, there are no publicists or teams to get through, and I read all my messages. It might take me a while to get back to you, but I will do my best to do so.

The address is:

MelanieStephens@mail.com

I look forward to meeting you!

Other books by the same author:

Isolation Tales

In 2020, the world suffered a global health crisis unlike anything else any of us had ever seen. As well as bringing fear, the contagion brought unity and solidarity within countries and whole nations came together. This compilation of short stories covers several aspects of the potentially deadly infection and humankind at this time. An eclectic mix of uplifting, moving, funny and thought-provoking tales revealing different perspectives of this period. Inspired by real accounts and interviews, this collection includes stories of keyworkers, children, supermarket panic buyers, stay at home mums, even the disease itself among others. It provides a well-rounded experience of this memorable chapter and the unmistakable spirit of the human race. All profits from sales of this book are being donated to the National Health Service in the UK.

The Collection

Highly anticipated, The Collection, brings together for the first time a treasury of work by Cornish author, Melanie Stephens. Known for her relatable storytelling and compelling writing style, this anthology features 75 stories, poems, and articles personally chosen and arranged by the author herself. This selection includes several pieces of brand-new work never seen before, exclusive to this publication. According to the author, this is her most definitive showcase to date and encompasses personal experiences amongst a varied display of works that shaped the writer she is today. Featuring talked about favourites such as 'Stolen Moment', 'Woman', and 'Be Careful what you Search For', the pieces range from laugh-out-loud funny to thrilling, tear-jerking and thought-provoking. This edition of the collection also features introductions, and photographs from the author's personal collection to accompany the works. **Also available in Special Edition**

Printed in Great Britain
by Amazon

84250195R00102